The Gift

First Published in Great Britain 2012 by Netherworld Books
an imprint of Belvedere Publishing

Copyright © 2012 by Tegon Maus

All rights reserved. No part of this publication may be reproduced or transmitted, in any form or by any means, without permission of the publishers or author. Excepting brief quotes used in reviews.

First edition: 2012

Any reference to real names and places are purely fictional and are constructs of the author. Any offence the references produce is unintentional and in no way reflects the reality of any locations or people involved.

A copy of this work is available through the British Library.

ISBN : 978-1-909224-07-0

Netherworld Books
Mirador
Wearne Lane
Langport
Somerset
TA10 9HB

THE GIFT

THE CHRONICLES OF TUCKER LITTLEFIELD

TEGON MAUS

Acknowledgements

To my wife Dearheart... without who's help this book would have never been written.

To my friend and Mentor Terri Valentine without who's help this book would never have been read.

To my new friend Sarah Luddington without who's help this book would never have been published.

And to my friend Diana who always gave her honest opinion.

Prologue

Transformed by a primitive magic beyond a civilized man's understanding, I was given a horrible gift that no man should possess... It held me, twisted me, turning me at its bidding. I was enslaved by its power, compelled to devour the souls of the dead until I became the monster of my fears.

I have seen things I wish never to see again. I have done things of which I wish never to speak. Yet I must if I am to find the answers to fulfill my hope.

I have walked upon blue ribbons of molten stone to peer into the depth of a man's soul.

I watched as a promise made at birth brought my friend Enon to sacrifice everything to become whole again – all in an effort to save the life of his child.

I have cried without shame for the loss of all I hold dear and for fear that the future will hold more than I can bear.

I am Tucker Littlefield. Know all that I say now is true-spoken.

I pushed hard at the large wooden door. It swung open with a well-worn groan. Stepping inside, I drew a deep breath, my lungs filling with the pungent smells of wood smoke and ale, which hung in the air of all good taverns. Massive beams, rooted in the floor, rose high into the rafters, spreading their branches like outstretched arms and holding the roof as high as any basilica. The broad tables, wooden chairs, and wide plank floor, all scuffed with years of use, were like old friends to me.

"Evening, sir, I'm so happy to see you."

"And I you, Toby," I said, hanging up my coat.

"How is your wife this fine night?"

"It isn't polite, Toby, to ask about the welfare of the Devil in a house of worship," I said sternly.

"Sorry, sir. I meant no offense," he said wryly, just as he always did.

At fourteen, he played the game well.

"None taken, my boy, none taken," I said, patting him on the shoulder before I headed to my usual table. "Now then, my young friend, big fish? Little fish? How large a net do we cast tonight?"

"A large one, to be sure. There are people here from seven townships for the telling," he said with his usual enthusiasm.

"Seven, you say?" I asked playfully, secretly happy for the news.

"Aye, sir, seven," he beamed.

"Alright then, a large one it is. Now go tell your father I'm here," I said, pulling the chair out to make myself comfortable. On the table, a folded piece of paper with my name, Tucker Littlefield, written in bold red letters, held my place.

Shortly, the sound of heavy footsteps pounded their way out of the kitchen to greet me.

"Tucker," Jack's voice boomed out before he reached my table.

"Jack," I said, standing, offering my hand.

"Where's the Devil hiding this night? Not far behind, I'll wager," he said, pumping my arm vigorously.

"Upon my very coattails, my friend, always but a few steps behind," I joked.

"Well, let's hope she doesn't find you until after the telling," he said, slapping me hard on the back.

"Toby said there are some from as far away as seven townships," I said weakly.

"A few. Maybe one or two a little farther."

"Well, we'll see then, won't we?"

"Who knows, my friend, maybe one of them will have news."

"Stranger things, I suppose," I said.

"Only good things tonight, huh? At least until the Devil catches you here," he said, trying to change my mood.

I nodded in agreement. My mind spun with the thought.

"Something to eat?" he asked.

"Sure, a little something," I replied.

"Big fish, little fish," he said with a weak smile and returned to the kitchen.

"Big fish, little fish," I called after him.

Chapter 1

"A Jonda?" The man roared with laughter. "It's not possible. You, sir, are the best liar I have ever had the misfortune of meeting."

"Please, you flatter me," I said with a slight nod. Another man might have taken offense at such a remark, but for me this was high praise, indeed. "I could never invent a story to compete with this truth."

"A commoner? A giant with a dog, no less trusted above all others by a King," the man said, standing and waving his flagon for emphasis as he spoke.

The tavern exploded with laughter. The twenty or so people present had given me their undivided attention.

Nothing could make me happier, the larger the audience the better.

"I assure you," I said, rising slowly, smoothing my hand over my balding head, readying myself. I caught Jack's eye and nodded slightly toward the man at the head of the table. The man followed my gaze to him and smiled to himself, shaking his head. His hand waved loosely, beckoning Jack closer.

"All he can drink, Innkeeper and the money, sir, until we can catch him in a lie," he said firmly to Jack and tossed a leather bag upon the table.

"I assure you," I started again, "this tale is no lie. Enon Tutelo exists and the Kingdom of Irkland and I are the better for it."

My glass newly filled, I stood on the table, nodded my appreciation to my new patron and waited for silence. The net had been cast.

"Let me think, my friends. Where do I start?" I took a long draw from the glass and then waved it slightly to signal I was ready for another. Jack filled it to overflowing. "Ahh, it's coming to me now. The beginning, the day he came into the world. Well, I think it best we are honest with one another. All you have heard about his birthright is true."

A soft gasp escaped from several women closest to my

table. I took the opportunity to empty my glass once more.

"Fault him not for being born the son of a witch, nor for being Jonda. He had no more choice than you or I."

Harsh whispers floated softly among the crowd.

"There are those who say..." I looked deep into the bottom of my glass and swirled it slowly. "Well, we would have to ask ourselves whom the Goddess would look more harshly upon, he or the cowards who... " I paused for effect, pulling a chair to the tabletop and sat down, surveying each face that waited silently for my next words.

Wood smoke hung in the air like morning fog as Jack crept behind me to fill my cup once more.

"It happened this way," I said, drawing a deep breath and reaching for my glass. "Her name was Sara; alone, pregnant, no man of name in her life. She was a seventh generation practitioner, raised in the Sisterhood from childhood. Beaten and robbed by three men for a necklace, thought to hold the power of her religion. It was but a trinket, handed down from mother to child upon coming of age, and held no power beyond this. From fear of her power or cruelty for its own sake, they stabbed her several times."

"Come along now. This is not the story we bargained for." My patron shifted uncomfortably, and the audience grumbled their agreement.

"My apologies, dear friends, it is not my desire to be vulgar or to shock you, but it is important we all understand what has made a man become the likes of Enon Tutelo. My point is this. Not all witches are bad and not all men are good. She, like you or I, had but one thought at the end: the well being of her unborn child."

An uncomfortable silence hung thick in the air. I sipped at my glass patiently.

"Left for dead," I began again, "she was found by one of her own. But the damage was too great and only one life could be saved - hers or the child's. As her life drained from her, she begged her companion to save the child and for one last thing, a promise that her child never be alone." I wiped my eyes with the back of my hand and emptied my glass.

"Goddess knows, there is nothing more powerful than a mother's love, be she witch or mortal, nothing stronger in all of creation. Her companion complied and Enon Tutelo was brought into the world, baptized in his dead mother's blood. As he drew his first breath, the Goddess's mark was placed upon him. A cut on the right side of his neck, gained at the very moment the dagger was plunged, taking his mother's life. To heal the wound, to keep the promise, her companion performed the rights. With lightning, with fire, and a silver dagger, with words of magic known only to those who have practice of those beliefs, the child was saved. And to the promise, it was kept all too well, cleaved with that bolt of lightning. Enon Tutelo would never be alone. I ask only that you hold this image, only for a while, just until I make myself clear. This man, my friends, was both blessed and cursed that night. Had it been any one of us and we were given the choice forced upon him at birth, I wonder how many of us would accept his particular gift. Let me leave it at this... Enon Tutelo is a good man, as good as any man here."

I rocked my chair back softly, waiting for their reaction. I ran my finger absentmindedly over the silver chain attached to my vest. Counting the links allowed me to adjust for the timing. Content with their silence, I knew they were mine.

"Now then," I said, snapping the legs of the chair on the tabletop with a loud crack. "That said, we can move on," I allowed my voice to become buoyant and everyone gave a collective sigh of relief. I emptied my glass, and tossed it to Jack.

"I was a guest of a particular Nobleman," I said, standing, holding out my hand to halt any who would ask for a name. "Who shall remain nameless in deference to his sister, who found my presence, shall we say, charming."

A small sprinkling of laughter made its way around my audience. I took that moment to survey the room; a few more tables had found occupants.

"You may make of that what you will." I smiled, winking at the women closest to me. My glass had been returned and refreshed. I settled myself again. "My patron had been invited to enjoy the king's generosity and, thanks to his sister, so was I. A gala of grand proportions, a wonderful affair, the Queen's birthday, I think." I leaned back in the chair and fondled the pipe in my pocket. "The music was wonderful. The music," I repeated softly, removing my pipe. I slipped the chain from my pocket. At its end, a small leather pouch held the true nature of story telling, Jonda tobacco.

I began to fill the pipe and lit it, puffing gently. Soft clouds of blue smoke rose from it to drift over them all, mixing with the ever present wood smoke... big fish and little fish. "Better," I whispered to myself. As my voice rose, the smoke floated higher and then began to change color. It swirled, gaining density. A faint blue light surged through it, coming alive with the images of which I spoke. A sudden rush of whispers filled the room, followed closely by laughter and then all-out applause as those images came to life within the body of that blue smoke. They danced and pulsated with the rhythm of my voice.

"People of every color, every description, from every corner of the kingdom, Goddess what an event! I've never had an evening like it before, or since. Present company excluded, of course. Marble floors shining so bright one could comb one's hair in the reflection. There were so many candles, it turned night into day. And the food, the dancing, the music. Goddess, it was a night I'll never forget. It was the first time I laid eyes on Enon Tutelo.

"More than a three hundred people filled the enormous room. All cleared a path as he entered. The music, the laughter, all sound, slowly gave way to his presence like water poured onto a fire. A hiss of whispers filled the void of his passing. I had never seen anything of the like before. They moved out of his way as if he carried the plague. And then as he was closest to them, they turned their backs and pretended he wasn't there. An impossible pretense, I assure you.

"He stood a full head taller than any man there. His shoulders were as wide as a table, his arms thick as a man's leg, rippling with muscles beyond the ordinary, cabled with thick veins, a true Jonda from head to toe. His hair, black as coal, hung below his shoulder blades and my friends, as if that were not enough, he wore it in a tail like a single woman or a widow. But who are we to question the ways of those stranger than ourselves? There is more, much more. Around his neck, hung a silver chain, much like this one," I said, holding my tobacco pouch for all to see.

"Strung upon it, three claws, a larger encompassed by two smaller, each separated by a blue stone. They were curved, white, and still as sharp as a new knife. I shudder to think of the creature from which they were taken. I later discovered it was a token to mark his passage into manhood. A story I would be happy to tell some other night.

"He wore a deep red tunic covered by a blue vest. With black pants and boots, he was completely underdressed for such a grand occasion.

"At first, I thought this the reason for his rude treatment. I was wrong. By his side, matching his stride was a dog the likes of which I have never seen. It was unnaturally large, with shoulders as square as Enon's, and as black as night. Only the white star at its forehead and a white swath under its chin broke its color.

"The two walked as if they were the only ones in the room, ignoring guards and noblemen alike, right up to the King himself."

"Sire," he said with bold formality. No bow, no moment of humble gesture. As fate would have it, he and his dog stopped directly across from me.

I was overcome with the feeling, how do I describe it? The hair on the back of my neck stood straight up. I tried to shake it off, but this feeling filled me with increasing discomfort. The dog was staring at me. As our eyes met, a surge of goose bumps washed over me. It took two steps closer, its blue eyes locking on mine. My brain began to squirm inside my head, shifting ever so slightly as if making room for another person or another soul. As its stare drove deeper into me, my mind began to unfold, layer by layer like pages of a book. My life was being recalled one event after the other, exposing my innermost private of thoughts.

"Don't look at it." A hand pulled at my shoulder, trying to turn me away from the canine's glare. "For Goddess' sake, turn away," a voice whispered harshly in my ear.

The beast's stare penetrated my very soul, stripping away any defense I may have held. It was one with my mind. No thought, past or present, could be withheld from this brute, this dog. Enon slowly swung his head in my direction and the dog shifted his gaze to him. He lifted his chin slightly and the dog snorted and returned to his side.

"I see your sister has been up to her usual pranks," the King groaned softly to his wife.

"Be nice, dear," the Queen whispered in return.

"Sire, perhaps it would be best to discuss this in private," Chancellor Grimwell suggested, sending an unfavorable look in my direction. He was a tall, well-built man, impressed with his own importance. The finery of his clothing, his manner, his walk, even the way his beard was trimmed spoke of his position and what he thought of himself.

I was consumed by the little drama unfolding in front of me. It was as if I were suddenly invisible, privy to the petty squabbles of royalty. It had all the makings of a very interesting story.

"Sire," the Chancellor pressed, placing a hand on the king's forearm.

"You forget yourself," the King intoned flatly.

"Forgive me, Sire, I only meant... " Grimwell said, removing his hand.

The Queen pushed her way past the two men to stand in front of the giant.

"Mr. Tutelo," she said, turning a shoulder toward him as if measuring his height against her own. "My sister says you should be my husband's chancellor instead of Mr. Grimwell. What do you think?"

There was an uncomfortable silence. Grimwell visibly stiffened. Enon looked to the dog and the dog to him before answering.

"No, sister wrong. Enon not want Grimwell's job," he said, his voice deeply penetrating.

His words, their rhythm, their tone stunned me. It was like listening to a child. Here was a man, a giant of a man mind you, without fear of King or servant and his speech was broken, adolescent. I was held in the grip of the moment, mesmerized by the scene in front of me. I gaped openly.

"Really? She says no one can withhold the truth from you. You can see into their very souls and know if they are lying. Is that true?"

I was thunderstruck. She was describing exactly what had happened to me. It had to be true. I experienced it firsthand. I waited with excitement for his answer.

He said nothing.

"Your King awaits your answer," she prompted stiffly.

"Sister wrong, Enon not want job," he repeated.

"Sire, your guest," Chancellor Grimwell said, "perhaps... "

Someone tapped my shoulder. It was my paramour. Smiling, she knew my interest almost better than I. She drew my attention to the woman across the room, the Queen's sister Ruthie, whose expression spoke volumes. She was about to take someone to task.

"Sister, please don't torment my guest," she called from halfway across the room and rushed to intervene, protocol be damned.

Enon's manner changed almost immediately. He shifted his weight several times and his face flushed with a wide smile. He lowered his head, giving Ruthie a slight bow as she rushed to stand in front of him.

"I see you've met my sister Gwen," she said matching his smile. "And the King, of course," she added abruptly, having forgotten herself and nodded her respect as quickly as possible.

"It used to mean something, being King," his Highness teased.

"Yes, Enon met nice people. How Izie?" He asked, taking hold of her hand.

"Elizabeth is fine. She's waited all day just to see you," she said, leaning closer before she led him to a nearby alcove.

"I wasn't done, Ruthie," the Queen admonished and followed them.

The King, with a deep sigh, rolled his eyes and trailed along.

Hidden behind heavy red drapery that framed the alcove from prying eyes stood a young girl of seven or so...

"Truth-seeker," she said excitedly, bowing playfully, holding her right fist over her left shoulder.

"Pure-heart," Enon intoned seriously and returned her salute before picking her up in his huge arms.

"Ruthie," Queen Gwen whispered, leaning forward to nudge her sister.

"Sire, this is most irregular," Chancellor Grimwell protested. "This charlatan has no right to be here."

"He is not a charlatan," Princess Ruth barked.

"Ruthie, please," her sister prodded. "After all, he is a Jonda."

"I don't care. He's good, he's honest and he loves..." Ruthie stopped in mid-sentence. Panic overshadowed her face as she looked to her sister and then to Enon. She placed her hands on his chest and leaned into him before taking the child. "Show them, Enon. Show them who you really are."

The room held its collective breath. Enon stood motionless.

So much was happening so fast, I hadn't realized I had lost track of my companion.

A faint mumbling of voices filtered into my awareness. As I looked about, everyone present had turned their backs to the King and his wife. They had begun to make mindless chattering noises in some pretense the royal conversation was not happening. I was so engrossed in this royal drama; I didn't notice the dog sitting in front of me. Nor that those standing closest to me had silently moved away, leaving me standing alone.

"Him Tucker," Enon, still looking at the floor, spoke up. "Born moocher, liar, hand in other man's pocket," he muttered.

I was stunned. He knew my name, although he was wrong on all other counts.

"A transparent observation, even for a Jonda, he probably heard his name earlier in the evening. Besides, everyone here knows Mr. Littlefield's reputation," Chancellor Grimwell scoffed.

All five turned to look at me. The dog sat sentinel in front of me.

"Perhaps, I can help," I offered, bowing. "Mr. Tutelo's observations are, at best, the reflection of overheard conversations, the seeds of jealousy or envy for my personal abilities, perhaps. Please feel free to look into my mind, if that is indeed what you do. I will pick a number between one and ten."

A light titter of laughter rewarded my personal vanity. At that moment I held visions of an extended stay within those magnificent walls and stepped closer.

Enon glanced at the dog and then at me.

"Good dog," I said and bent to pet the creature. I was met with an immediate gasp from the crowd and a very convincing growl from the dog. Slowly, I pulled my hand back.

"I see he doesn't like strangers," I quipped.

"Go on, Enon, read him," Ruthie prompted.

"Let me make it easier for you," I said, stepping back. I placed my hand on my head and pretended to concentrate.

The dog stared intently at me. I tried my best to ignore it and shifted a little so it couldn't look directly into my face. It didn't matter. I could feel its heated gaze, boring into me, peeling away all efforts to keep it from my most private of thoughts. I could not. It sorted quickly through my less than proud moments.

It saw every instance of which I had turned a moment of virtue to my personal advantage, and it filled me with no small level of shame.

It was the most ghastly, most revealing feeling one could possibly imagine, much like the end time will be, standing in front of the Goddess herself, accounting for one's life and the way one lived it before going on to the next. I had hoped never to be filled with that feeling again, at least not while living. The dog snorted, turned away and returned to his master's side.

"Dog hear before. Story not funny," Enon scoffed and turned to Ruthie before I could say a word, and all dreams of being the King's guest drowned in their laughter.

I stood embarrassed and bewildered, trying to think of something to say to escape this particular limelight.

The dog suddenly spun and tensed. It exchanged a brief look with Enon and then was off on a dead run.

"Safe here. Not move," Enon ordered before following.

Suddenly, several women screamed and the room fell into chaos. Someone was fighting. The King's guards appeared instantly and formed a protective circle around him. The retreating crowd pushed me into the alcove along with the royal family. There was horrible shouting and the chilling sounds of battle.

"Cayra." The Jonda word for freedom rose above all other sounds. There were too many people in front of me to see clearly.

More guards appeared in an attempt to squelch the fighting. Shortly, the conflict reached the alcove. The people in front of me parted like a curtain. Five Jonda fought at the center of the turmoil.

They were huge, a full foot taller than Enon himself. Each wielded a long knife with a thick blade and turned it repeatedly. They stood, shirtless, shoulder to shoulder, forming a wall of flesh that heaved in unison. Their long black hair was tied in a ball at the back of their heads with a slip of red cloth, their faces smeared with paint. All but a few of the King's men lay sprawled on the floor at their feet. Enon and his dog was the only barrier between them and the King.

"Brother, we have no wish to harm you. Stand aside," one said.

"Not harm any," Enon said his voice low and menacing. His dog stood to his right, braced for a sign from his master to attack.

My heart pounded wildly in my chest. The blood thumped loudly in my ears. I was sure it could be heard by all.

"Why Jonda here?" Enon asked, shifting his weight. His dog inched forward a step.

The one closest to him spoke in their native tongue; angry words filled with hate.

"Speak words all understand. Jonda have no secrets here," Enon replied. His fingers flexed involuntarily, eager for the fight.

"Our brothers, your brothers, are held as slaves. Their souls ripped from their bodies to become the undead. We come to free them, and to make an example of their keeper." The man's words were just as angry as they had been in his native tongue.

"This man king... good king... not know words you speak. He not keep Jonda," Enon countered.

"Lies, he holds them just as he holds you, his lap dog."

"He is Enon Tutelo, the truth-seeker," Elizabeth said, pushing her way to the front of the adults to stand right in front of the Jonda.

Enon reached out to pull the child back as his dog slid between her and the danger that stood only inches away. The few remaining guards pressed the King and Queen against the back wall to protect them with their bodies.

Queen Gwen grasped wildly at her sister and frantically whispered her name.

Ruthie pressed hard against Enon's back, twisting her fist

in his tunic and clutching at the air, inches short of dragging Elizabeth to safety. The young girl held no fear of the Jonda or of her mother.

At that moment I saw an opportunity beyond imagining. If I could pull the child to safety, the King's gratitude could last a lifetime.

Slowly, I came to realize that my feet had taken on a will of their own I was moving forward. Ruthie clutched at my shoulder as I glided by her in a fog.

"Gentleman," I heard the word and was stunned. It was my voice. I picked up Elizabeth and started to turn.

"Take it back. Take what you said about Enon back, or you'll be sorry," she said, struggling in my arms and shaking her fist at them.

"Citizen, would you hide behind a child?" The Jonda voice came again, openly irritated by her taunts.

"He's not afraid of you either," Elizabeth spit out, trying to escape my grip.

My feet stopped and turned me to face them.

"Is this true, Citizen? Do you hold no fear?"

"No fear." My mouth wouldn't listen to my brain. That wasn't what I wanted to say. I was very afraid, but high reward came from high risk. My heart pounded so hard I thought it would burst out of my chest.

My feet began to move again, turning me. Ruthie held her arms out to take Elizabeth from me. As the child passed from my grip to hers, the Jonda word 'Cayra' rang in my ears and I was struck in the back, driven to the ground.

As I fought to hold onto consciousness my ears were filled with the fierce sounds of fighting and the screams of Elizabeth and her mother. I lay on the floor, showered in blood.

I was kicked, beaten by the weight of people falling on top of me.

The harrowing sound of that dog and the unmerciful carnage it dispensed filled the air.

Goddess forgive me, I was afraid... so afraid I lay on the floor in a puddle of my own fear and waited to be killed... or worse yet, found by the dog.

Chapter 2

My head swam. I struggled to open my eyes and there before me, an angel.

"Back among the living, are we?" A strange female voice asked.

I searched the room for anything familiar. It was dark and unyielding. A candle flickered on the stand next to the bed I lay upon. The covers were smooth, warm, and extraordinarily clean.

"Can you hear me, Mr. Littlefield?" the angel asked.

"Where am I? Who are you?" I asked.

Her face was round and attractive. Her hair was silver, with skin as smooth as a baby's. She appeared to be five, perhaps six years my elder.

"Mr. Littlefield, listen to my voice," she snarled, grabbing me, pulling me upright in the bed. Her face filled with sudden loathing and hovered inches from my own. "Are you listening, Mr. Littlefield?"

I nodded weakly, my eyes open in full bewilderment. My angel had suddenly become a fiend.

"Good. First, my Mistress and the King think you a hero. But I know you, Tucker Littlefield. There is talk of you, and I, for one, believe every word. I will not let you worm your way into this house or that of the King. Do we understand each other, Mr. Littlefield?"

"No, I'm sure there must be some misunderstanding. I... "

"Let me make it perfectly clear. They have my baby and you will bring her back," she said, yanking the covers, forcing me to tumble out of the bed to the floor.

"Who is they?" I asked, trying to collect myself.

"Those Jonda, Mr. Littlefield. They have Elizabeth. Those cowards used her as a shield to escape. Enon followed them."

"Good, if anyone can bring her back, I would think it to be him." I pulled the blankets from the floor and tried to assemble the bed and return to its comfort.

"Oh, no you don't. You have two days to reach Bridgehaven."

"You must be insane. I would have to ride night and day to make Bridgehaven in two days. Besides, I have no interest in going anywhere," I said, slipping under the covers again.

"Really? Let me tell you your future, Mr. Littlefield. In less than five minutes one of the King's guards will be here to check on your well being. The King wishes to give his personal thanks on behalf of my mistress. When he arrives, I will tell him I overheard you talking in the garden with the Jonda leader before their attack."

"You *are* insane. I never saw a Jonda before last night, nor have I ever been in the King's garden." I couldn't hide the panic in my voice.

"Under the circumstances, sir, who do you think the King will believe? Chancellor Grimwell has convinced the King that Enon was involved, part of a plan to kill him. He has convinced him that Enon allowed them to take Elizabeth so he could escape unsuspected. The King has given Grimwell full responsibility do whatever it takes, whatever he wants, to retrieve her. All Jondas are to be arrested or killed on sight if they resist, until she is returned."

"My Goddess, woman, what does all this have to do with me?"

"If Grimwell gets the chance he will kill Enon and my Ruthie loves him. Such sorrow could only be surpassed by the loss of Elizabeth.

I will not allow that to happen. I will do anything to save them, even if I have to sell my soul to the devil, and, Mr. Littlefield, yours as well."

"Why involve me? I've done nothing to deserve such ire."

"You have the King's favor. You will go and save my Elizabeth or I will see to it you never sit at a table in this realm again. I will be there to slap every mug of ale from your hand before it reaches your lips. I will make your name as dark a word as the plague. I will spread it to the very edge of the world and back again if you fail me."

Softly, there came a knock at the door. I stared at it as if the Dark Lord himself waited on the other side. This woman glared at it and then at me. Her chest heaved and her nostrils flared in an unnatural manner. My heart had jumped to my throat and I could not swallow.

"You are an evil woman," I whispered harshly, suddenly

filled with anger. "Evil, pure and simple, just evil."

The knock came a second time.

"Pray, sir, you never have need to find out how evil. You have seen but a blade of grass in a whole world of fields," she hissed and yanked the covers, pulling me to the floor again.

"Come in," she called after a third knock, making no effort to disguise the irritation in her voice.

"Sorry, Governess, the King is asking for Mr. Littlefield again," a guard said, poking his head into the room.

For a moment, I had visions of escape, of salvation from this harridan. He didn't look at her; he just stared at the floor. His face twitched with fear. His eyes darted nervously as if looking for an escape. He was more afraid of her than me, and my heart sank. His frightened expression brought me to full belief of her threats. I hung my head in resignation.

"Tell the King he will be there shortly," she ordered firmly.

He nodded and quickly scampered away, happy in his retreat.

"Get dressed, Mr. Littlefield. Enon will be waiting for you in Bridgehaven."

"But the King... " I stuttered.

"I'll make your apologies for you," she said sternly.

"Goddess, how did I ever get here? Do you have a name? If you're going to haunt the balance of my life, I'll need a name, I would like to curse it," I asked, suddenly filled with disappointment.

"Eloise, Governess Eloise, Elizabeth's nanny. I was her mother's nanny as well. Mr. Littlefield, the King will probably give you, I don't know, something. But my Elizabeth, my baby, I will give you anything, everything. She may be Ruthie's child, but she is, Mr. Littlefield, she is my daughter. Have I made myself clear?"

"Perfectly," I replied, fingering the edge of the sheets, hoping to return to their comfort.

"Bring her home and I promise you, you will never have to work another day for the rest of your life. Ale will flow like water, food will have no end and you can sleep to your heart's content."

"Really?" I asked, wanting to believe.

"It's the best I can do to balance the scales, Mr.

Littlefield," she said. Her shoulders slumped as if in defeat. Her face suddenly looked worn, with deep furrows dividing her forehead. Worry had taken its toll on her pleasant face.

"How is Princess Ruth?" I asked, hoping she wouldn't start to cry. I could handle the threats, the anger, anything but crying.

"Devastated. They found her this morning, wandering in the forest, half dressed, half crazy with grief, calling Elizabeth's name."

The tone of her voice stabbed at my heart, pushing it to my throat. There was nothing I could say.

"Get ready. I'll be back shortly," she whispered, fighting back her tears.

I nodded softly and did as she asked, seeking my clothes in the darkness. I sat on the bed to pull on my boots and sank in its comfort. It beckoned to me and my body sought to answer its call, but my mind raced with images of the Jonda and of Elizabeth.

For the first time, I looked about the room. It wasn't very large but well-appointed. The furniture of rich cherry wood reflected the candle's light and the dying embers in the hearth. The walls were an array of dark stones, worn with time and the many lives that had passed through the room. As I sat at the end of the bed, I saw that the wall facing me was littered with parchment, the creations of a child, some from Elizabeth, and some from Ruthie.

Flowers tied in bundles with sewing thread, hung upside-down from the ceiling, adding to the room's aroma. It was a pleasant, soft mixture of wood smoke and perfume. Somehow it fit this woman. The room spoke volumes of the love she held for both Elizabeth and the child's mother. I liked it here. It was safe, warm.

"Ready, Mr. Littlefield?" Eloise asked, pushing the door open quietly.

"I suppose I am," I answered.

She lit a candle and gestured for me to follow her. We passed through several corridors and finally through the kitchen.

Four pleasantly plump women, dressed in gray blue tunics and crisp white aprons, paused in their work to touch my arm and shoulder as we passed. They wiped their faces of tears and nodded their encouragement to me without saying a word.

I followed her outside, where the air was cold and damp. We made our way through the darkness to the stables.

A young man held the reins of the most beautiful horse I had ever seen. Steam bellowed from its nostrils as it stomped the ground, eager for the ride.

"Take this. You'll need it," she said, handing me an envelope.

"What is it?" I asked.

"A letter, Mr. Littlefield. It's an open hand from the King himself. It says you are on the King's business. His money is your money; his authority is your authority."

I was shocked. My head swam. Suddenly, the weight of the world settled on my shoulders. I hesitated to take it. If I did...

"Take it, Mr. Littlefield. With it you become a hero, or in two days it becomes your death warrant. It's your choice." Her voice trembled before trailing off.

"I don't want it. I really don't," I protested.

"You will, I promise," she said, slipping it into my coat pocket.

I pretended it wasn't there. I tried not to look into her face as I mounted the horse.

"His name is Escalan, sir. No finer beast exists in the entire Kingdom. He belongs to the King himself," the young boy said with pride.

I barely heard him speak. I don't know what made me look at her. I told myself I didn't want to. I only needed to ride into the darkness and I wouldn't have to see her face. Her tears reflected the candlelight as she looked up at me. Her face, round and flawless, was angelic again.

"Go to the eighth bridge. Enon will be there. If you're not, I'll know, Mr. Littlefield, and hell itself won't be able to hide you," she threatened softly.

"Wish me luck," I said.

"With all my heart," she whispered.

The horse exploded into the night and I let the darkness overtake me. I tried to convince myself that this was all a dream, a terrible, terrible dream. But the tears burning my face and the rustle of the paper in my pocket made it all too real.

The constant pounding of the horse's hooves drummed deep into my head, repeating itself over and over, Bridgehaven... Bridgehaven... Bridgehaven.

Chapter 3

Bridgehaven, the thought of it... How do I find a Jonda that doesn't want to be found? How do I find a little girl I've seen only once? The closer I got to Bridgehaven the more the questions haunted me. Night became day and then night crept upon me once more. Failure loomed larger with each footfall from my horse. It ran with heart, with the same desire that filled me, certain Eloise had chosen poorly.

I loved this little town. I had spent a considerable amount of time here in my youth. At one time I had visions of settling down, raising a family, and getting a dog.

I had to laugh a little to myself as Enon's dog jumped to mind. The neighbors would have loved that.

I stopped at the top of the last rise overlooking the town. It was just after sunset and the cooking fires glowed through a thousand windows.

Set in the middle of the Ekimi River, Bridgehaven was a beautiful hamlet, revered for its twelve huge bridges. Built from massive beams a thousand years ago, they reflected a time when craftsmen were given free rein. The fretwork, a symbolic representation of our creation, defied duplication even to this day.

The road divided in three directions, and as it began to rain, I strained my memory to locate the eighth bridge. My horse stomped nervously as I tried to make up my mind. Something had him spooked.

Movement caught my eye, rustling in the darkness along side the road I had finally chosen to follow. The hair on the back of my neck stood straight up. My horse pulled against my restraining hand, fighting to take another route. Again the crinkle of leaves cut through the soft rain and my horse stopped in the middle of the trail, frozen with fear. A hundred yards ahead a dark form crossed the road. Its yellow eyes flashed in my direction making my skin rippled with fear.

I pulled on the reins to hold my place as the apparition came closer. The horse reared up and dropped me to the ground before disappearing into the darkness.

"Citizen Tucker," the deep unmistakable voice offered its greeting.

"Enon. I should have known it was you," I said.

The yellow eyes came closer, becoming his dog.

"Tucker late."

"Sorry, I got here as fast as I could," I groused. I was irritated, wet, muddy and embarrassed.

"Eloise say wait." He just stood there and made no effort to help me to my feet. "Enon wait."

"Ah, the Governess. Why are we here? Why Bridgehaven?" I asked, stumbling in the mud to get to my feet.

"Enon follow Jonda here."

"Elizabeth is here?"

"Izie here, then not."

"Well, where the hell is she?"

"Here, then not," he repeated.

"I'm sorry. I don't understand. Is she in Bridgehaven or not?"

"Tucker not want help Enon, say so." His animosity toward me showed through his voice. He turned his back and walked down the path. "Enon not need help. Dog help Enon find Izie. Citizen Tucker can go home," he said and waved his hand to dismiss me.

"I promised Governess Eloise to bring Elizabeth home safe to her mother. Not to mention you," I said angrily.

"Not mention Enon. Enon not need mention from Tucker. Enon know all Tucker can say." He turned and shook his finger at me.

"I only meant—"

"Not mention Enon. Last time say," he warned.

"Fine, have it your way. Come on, I know a little place where we can get something to eat." I started down the path toward town.

"Enon not hungry."

"Well, I am. So you can come or you can stay, but I'm cold, I'm wet, I'm tired and I'm hungry and I don't care anymore." I waited but he said nothing. I shook my head and turned again to go.

"Dog hungry, Enon go."

The town, although familiar, had changed since my last visit. The homes, all dressed in clapboard siding, made it confusing in the dark. Eventually, we made our way to the center of town to the Dores Inn. It was a small tavern with good food, a place to sleep, and sometimes, if lucky, a little something extra.

"Tucker? Tucker Littlefield is that you?"

"Anderson, I thought you would have sold this old dung heap before now, or the rats would've taken it over," I teased the innkeeper.

I hardly recognized him. It had been years since I had seen him last. Although Andy had never been a handsome man, time had been less than fair. His thin red hair had gone missing up the center and the wisps that remained stood at right angles to his head. His skin was blotchy and ruddy from years of drink. I seldom drank, but with him I was seldom sober.

"Hey, you. Get out," he suddenly yelled angrily as Enon slipped through the door behind me.

"Andy, he's with me," I soothed.

"We don't serve his kind here, Tucker."

"His kind? What the hell does that mean?"

"He's a stinking savage."

"What are you talking about? He's just a Jonda."

"And we don't serve his kind here."

"Andy, what the hell's gotten into you? I don't remember you being like this."

"Things change, Tucker, and I say he's out."

"I said he's with me. If you want, think of him as a bodyguard or whatever it takes, but he stays," I said firmly. No one, least of all Andy, was about to tell me what I could and couldn't do.

"I don't care who you say he is, get him out."

"Perhaps it would be best if I talked to you-know-who. I'm sure she would be interested in a little get-together I seem to remember."

"Keep her out of this, Tucker. She doesn't need to know anything about that. Besides, that was years ago. What's her name is married now... the blacksmith. He doesn't have much of a sense of humor. Best to leave the past in the past."

"Fine with me. We'll need a room and something to eat."

"I don't want any trouble here, Tucker. He so much as breaks wind I'm coming to you. Understand?"

"Yeah, I got it. Now, what do you say, a little bread, a little cheese, some meat, maybe a little ale?"

"Take the room at the top of the stairs. The kitchen is closed and no ale – not for you and certainly not for him."

"You're being a bastard, Andy. Now for the last time, I'm cold, I'm wet and I want something to eat. Please don't make my friends here get ugly."

"Alright, but you're both out of here at first light."

"Gladly, Andy. First light," I said and started up the stairs.

"No dogs allowed, Tucker."

"What dog?" I said, ignoring him.

"That dog. You can blackmail me into letting that heathen stay but not even you can have a dog in here."

"I don't have a dog," I said, turning to face him. Enon and his companion slipped up the stairs past me toward our room. "You gotta stop sampling the goods, Andy. You're seeing things."

"No trouble, Tucker. I mean it."

"No trouble, Andy."

The room held the smell of mildew but was warm. I sat next to the small hearth and crackling fire, trying to get the feeling back in my feet.

"Enon not bodyguard for Tucker."

"Look, if you don't want to sleep indoors, then don't. I don't care, but I need to sleep, even for a little while." I said and sat on the bed.

"Him not bring food," Enon said with an I-told-you-so tone.

"Yeah, I know," I said and lay out on the bed. "Put the candle in the window for me, will you?"

"No, bad thing. Tucker not do this," he said, standing.

"What? The candle? I've always slept with a candle in the window."

"Enon know. Enon know all things, Tucker. Bad thing now."

"You know all things, Tucker? What does that mean?" I asked, looking over my shoulder at him.

"Dog see inside Tucker; Enon see inside dog. Enon know all things, Tucker."

"All things? You couldn't possibly?" I asked with some dread and a lot of disbelief.

He stood there looking at me and my heart sank a little with the thought of his words. I glanced at the dog, which was still staring at me. I was overwhelmed with an instant of memory, a memory inside this very building. The images of my night with Andy's wife after I had set things in motion between him and the young lady, now the blacksmith's wife, filled my head. I turned away from the dog only to see Enon's face. His head cocked slightly to one side as if something inside him pitied me. A pang of guilt sliced through me as I turned away.

"Just put the candle in the window, please. You can blow it out after I fall asleep."

"Enon know Tucker afraid of dark."

"No, I'm not. It's just a habit, that's all. Afraid of the dark? Please." I rolled over and the eyes of the dog were staring me in the face.

I closed my eyes and tried to sleep. As I dozed and awoke the eyes were still there, fixed on me. Enon had spread himself across the floor, his back toward me. I leaned on one elbow to look at him. The dog shifted, leaning forward to match my curiosity. Enon made no movement to indicate he was awake or asleep. I lay back again and the dog eased its stance. I turned my back to the beast and fell asleep.

I was jolted awake when the dog jumped on my chest. My heart raced, and before I could yell, a huge hand covered my mouth.

"Tucker not move. No sound." He instructed.

It was everything I could do to breathe with the weight of the dog on me. Slowly, Enon moved away.

"Cayra, brother," his voice little more than a whisper.

"Cayra," a voice returned from the dark.

"Why here?" Enon asked.

"I saw your signal in the window. I came to free you, brother," the voice said.

I moved my head slowly in the direction of the voices. There, standing in the room, was another Jonda. I thought my heart would stop when something metal glinted in his hand.

"Not need saving, go with Enon's thanks."

"I heard this man say you are his servant. I saw your candle," the voice countered.

"Enon not slave. Tucker afraid of dark."

There was a long silence and then a controlled laughter from both men. The dog slowly slid off me and returned to its corner, its eyes locked on me once more.

They stood in the dark, speaking softly in their native tongue. The exchange went on for several minutes. I closed my eyes and tried to follow their conversation. It was fast, rhythmic, and interesting. The words carried a sense of familiarity between them. A commonality or central thread seemed to run through the words, binding them to each other and, I suppose, to all other Jonda.

With effort I opened my eyes, and to my surprise, those of the dog were closed. In the dark it was difficult to see the animal but I was certain, it was not looking at me. The oddity that stood out in my drowsy mind was Enon's voice. It was deep, strong and never hesitated, not even once. In his native tongue he was as eloquent as any statesman. The thought slowly sank into my mind and I rolled it over several times, trying to decide which end was up as I drifted off to sleep once more.

"Tucker." Enon's voice penetrated the thick fog of my consciousness.

"Go away. I'm sleeping."

"Not sleep. Trouble comes now."

"There will be plenty of trouble if I don't get some sleep soon," I said, pulling away from his grip.

"Trouble, now," he said forcefully yanking me to my feet.

The other Jonda was gone and we were alone. The sun was coming up. The sound of unruly voices filtered up the stairs to our room.

Andy and a few of his friends were coming and their voices grew louder. Enon's dog bristled and stood ready at the door.

"That's him," a strange man yelled, forcing the door open. Andy and three other men pushed their way into the room, inundating the air with the smell of drink.

"What the hell's going on here, Andy?"

"This bastard wiped out Caldron," the man in the door slurred.

"What? When did he do this?" I asked.

"Four days ago. A band of twenty of these murdering Jonda bastards burned it to the ground. He was their leader."

"Well, it couldn't be him. I've been with him for the past two weeks. He's never left my side," I lied.

"Ya? Well, we're going to solve our little Jonda problem right now," one of the men yelled and lurched forward with a dagger.

A flood of thoughts poured through me. They meant to kill him; I could see it in their faces. I have much of which I am ashamed, but I couldn't stand aside for this. I couldn't just let them murder him.

I stepped in front of him to grab for the dagger when a horrible pain shot through my side.

The dog lunged and the others advanced on Enon, all within the confines of the tiny room.

Clutching my side, a warm, thick wetness suddenly oozed through my fingers. I was bleeding. The dagger meant for the Enon found me instead.

I cried out in anger and pain as I was knocked to the floor. The dog rushed to sit on me, pushing against me until I was wedged between its massive body and the wall.

It snarled and snapped viciously at the men as each came within range, but it refused to release me.

Enon picked them up and threw them around like rag dolls. Neither the fight nor the furniture lasted long.

"Tucker hurt bad?" he asked.

"Get him off me." I grimaced.

Enon made a quick gesture to the hound and I was freed from its weight. He had obeyed his master without as much as a word between them.

"Good blood. Must be good hole," he said, trying to remove my hand from the wound.

"It's not stopping," I said beginning to feel a little panicked. My life was slipping away with each passing moment.

"Tucker look Enon's eyes. Not look at blood. Enon fix... promise," he said and pulled me to him. He slipped an arm around my shoulders and then my legs, lifting me like a child.

I passed in and out of awareness and we were downstairs and then all at once, outside. Branches flashed by with large patches of bright sky and then more, so tight together that they blotted out the sun.

Time didn't exist. The warmth of my blood soaked my clothes. My breathing slowed and I was weak beyond description. The light swirled in my head changing solid objects to fluid blobs that oozed before us and then melted away.

Sleep pulled at my consciousness; fear pounded sluggishly at my heart. We were moving, jostling over the ground for what seemed like forever. I hurt more with each new jarring impact. Enon cradled me as he ran, and the light began to grow into darkness. I struggled with myself, angry, full of fight for fear of dying... and then bartered for that life and finally accepted my fate, allowing the growing darkness to take me.

At that moment, as if Enon had heard the thought, he stopped and laid me on the ground. It was warm and soft; the smell of crushed grass filled me.

A flicker of light formed in the center of my darkness, growing larger. Someone pulled at my clothes and then my wound.

The crackling sounds of fire assaulted me.

The smell of burning flesh filled me with new panic. My wound screamed a new level of pain into my brain... I was on fire.

Chapter 4

I awoke to the sweet smell of wood smoke and breakfast, surprised I had awoken at all. I lay on the ground next to a fire. On the opposite side a woman crouched, stirring a pot. Neither Enon nor his dog was anywhere to be seen. I struggled to sit up.

"Better if you lie still," the woman said with little interest.

I forced myself up and leaned against a nearby rock.

"Suit yourself," she said.

"Where's Enon?" I grimaced.

"Gathering firewood, he'll be back soon."

"I don't see his mangy dog anywhere."

She made no acknowledgment of my attempt at humor. We were in a clearing, surrounded by a thick stand of birch trees, invisible to the remainder of the world.

She continued to stir her pot. She was dressed in a pale tanned hide and around her neck a talisman of bone. Her long black hair flowed over her shoulders. It was braided at her temples and pulled back to keep the remainder from falling into her face. With a large bridge for a nose, high cheekbones and a round pleasant face, she was obviously Jonda.

"Where are we?" I asked, hoping to break the awkward silence.

"Enon is coming, Cowan. He can answer your questions."

"My name is Tucker, Tucker Littlefield, not Cowan," I said with a little irritation in my voice.

She said nothing, adding a dark powder to her pot.

"Tucker not speak her. Show respect," Enon said. He stood to my left with an armful of dead branches and as always his dog by his side.

"I meant no disrespect."

"She Shaman, Jonda medicine woman, Daneba, fix Tucker."

"With my thanks," I said with a nod of appreciation.

"Hear my words, Cowan. He is the truth-sayer," she said, pointing toward Enon. "His life is in your hands. Protect it as you would your own. If he dies while you possess his soul, he will never enter the land of his ancestors. He will walk the world in spirit until the end of time, invisible to all but you. I will send you to hell by my own hand before I will tolerate that." Her tone was condescending and her eyes held daggers for me.

"My name is Tucker, not Cowan," I protested again.

"It mean outsider, not one with Jonda," Enon whispered.

"What?" I asked, confused.

"You are Citizen Tucker, yes?" She asked harshly.

I nodded.

"Citizen means you are an equal among your people, recognized as are they in any land."

"Yes," I said with pride.

"Here, you are not equal, not a Citizen. You are not Jonda, you are an outsider. Here, you are the lesser being."

"If you feel that way, why did you save me?"

"I had no choice, you are his soul bearer. The law is the law, even for you, cowan," she spit out.

"I'm his what?"

"The Goddess had called to Enon. Her intention was to bring him home. Those men meant to kill him. You placed your life between Her and him, offering your soul for his. You took him away from Her. You are his soul bearer. His life is now your responsibility."

"Being stabbed? It was an accident. I wasn't trying to save him. I was trying to kick the shit out of Andy, and the other drunk stabbed me, nothing more."

"Tucker modest, save Enon from knife. Enon dead now not for Tucker," he said, slapping me hard on the shoulder. His broad smile beamed at me, nodding several times excitedly.

Even the dog seemed to have a smile on its face.

"Drink this, it will ease the pain," Daneba said, and scooped a dark liquid from the pot, handing it to me.

"It's alright, actually I feel pretty good," I said, waving off the smelly concoction.

"It's not for that pain, Cowan," she taunted.

"Tucker drink," Enon said sternly.

Daneba held the cup out to me and I took it tentatively. She threw more wood on the fire as she began to whisper to herself.

Enon held the bottom of the cup, insuring I drank all it had to offer. It was as bitter-tasting as it smelled.

Daneba's words had become a chant, growing in volume and speed. She threw armfuls of wood into the fire and the flames rose wildly higher. Her voice became a blur of words, reaching a fevered pitch. A wall of flames stood between us as the fire grew increasingly out of control. The heat was becoming unbearable and a harsh wind began to blow.

Daneba's image appeared as I dug my heels into the soft dirt, pushing away from the fire's intensity. I was shocked to discover she had stepped into the fire itself. She walked through the curtain of flames, carrying a dagger. Her voice was one shrill, continuous sound.

Enon mumbled the words she spoke as he bowed before her on one knee. He held his right hand out to her as she stepped through the fire to my side. She took it and plunged the dagger into it and then turned to me. I pushed hard against the rock but could go no farther.

She grabbed my right hand, holding it tightly. I was frozen with fear and could not escape. The dagger suddenly flashed in her hand and she drove it deep into my palm. I wanted to scream, but nothing came out of my mouth. If it did, it was drowned out by the wails of Enon's dog. It howled, pained as deeply as I, as the flames of the fires became fingers, rippling out to tear open the dog's chest. They responded to Daneba's voice, doing her bidding, and peeled layers of flesh, laying open bone and hide alike, exposing the animal's beating heart.

A second unholy scream filled the air, deeper, wilder than that of the creature laid open at my side. It was Enon, and all that had happened to the dog began to repeat itself with him.

He, still kneeling, screamed as his chest turned inside out, his beating heart exposed to my gaze.

I was next to be disemboweled by her spell. The tearing of cloth and the sizzle of the fire as it pulled open my skin was deafening. The snap of bone wrenched at my fear and as I looked down, there beat my own heart. Blood ran freely from the hole in Enon's hand. Daneba's chant gained volume as she collected it in a silver bowl and the wind blew harder. As she chanted and the fire licked out repeatedly toward me, she poured Enon's blood into the fresh wound in my palm and between my fingers. She raised the bowl higher and the blood that streamed from it thinned to a single strand.

The wind howled ever louder as the clouds darkened, deeper and deeper. Lightning flashed wildly overhead, coming closer with each new strike. Thunder roared, crushing the air, pushing me down tightly to the ground.

The fire strained to its limits, jumping to me and then suddenly to Enon's heart and that of the dog. Both screamed in agony, as did I. The howl of that wind shrieked louder, drowning out the others. Pain racked every inch of my body.

I was overwhelmed with all that was taking place about me and then she did the unthinkable. She summoned from each, a wisp of themselves, their spirits, their souls, tore free from them to enter me through the hole in my palm.

A stir of Enon's mind filled me, for a moment, a rush of memories and images not my own.

For that instant I was engulfed with anguish, a loneliness that reached far beyond my own. The images of his life raced by in torrents, every pain, every rejection from his people as well as mine. I was overwhelmed, filled with the images of every soul he had seen into. Every life, every lie, every deceit, every ugly thing man and Jonda alike had tried to hide from him, even my own. He was an outcast in both societies, befriended by none and yet his sorrow was for them all.

My mind was pulled to Daneba once more as the lightning flashed wildly in response to her chanting, reaching an eerie pitch.

She stood over me as I thrashed upon the ground, the fire jumping from place to place on my body as it did with Enon and the dog. Daneba stepped full weight on my hand, pinning it to the ground. From behind her, she produced a branding iron, glowing orange with heat.

"Remember my words, Cowan," she yelled over the sounds in which I drowned, and drove the iron into my palm.

The sizzle of my searing flesh filled my ears. I was in shock and horrible pain. She removed her foot, releasing me. In my palm, three small symbols held within a circle sealed my wound.

"Cayra," she screamed and pointed at me. Thunder exploded in my ears as lightning reached down from the sky to envelop and consume me.

My heart stopped and I fought to draw breath.

"Goddess!" I cried, sucking in all the air my lungs could hold and sat up.

"Tucker sleep good?" Enon asked.

The fire, now little more than a small pile of ashes and glowing embers, spoke nothing of the inferno it had been just moments before.

"Daneba, the fire, the lightning," I muttered.

"Daneba gone two days now. Tucker sleep long time."

My mind swirled with the images of Daneba and her words, all gone now.

"Let me see your hand," I demanded.

"Why Tucker want see hand?"

"Just show it to me," I demanded impatiently.

He held his hand out to me. It held no mark, no blemish; no sign of Daneba's knife work. I was afraid to look at my own, afraid what might truly be there or, perhaps, not.

I turned my head away. Sitting several feet to my left was the dog, his eyes, as always, fixed on me. I dropped my gaze, moving it from the beast to my closed fist. I didn't want to know but knew I had to. Slowly, as my hand opened, my heart jumped. There in the center of my palm were the three symbols within the circle, just as before.

"Look," I said weakly to Enon, holding out my hand to him.

He shifted uneasily as he glanced at my hand.

"Soul bearer," he said simply and then went back to what he was doing.

"What happened to me?"

"Enon said... Soul bearer, nothing more."

"Nothing more? What happen to me? Why did you save me?"

He shifted once more, studying my face.

"Enon see all things inside Tucker," he said, squirming uncomfortably, as did I. "Enon not see in Tucker to want save Enon."

I didn't know what to say. Still the dog's eyes burned deeply into my consciousness.

"Where's Daneba?" I said, trying to change the subject.

"Enon said... gone. Tucker make ready now. Time to go."

"Go where? Do you know where Elizabeth is?"

"Yes, close now. Not safe here."

"Not safe? Why not?"

"She who hunts comes for us. Be ready, leave soon," he said, throwing my bedroll at me.

I held it for a moment, pressing it against my chest. I ran my fingers over it, seeking for any sign that would offer proof of my disembowelment.

"Who did you say was looking for us?" I asked absentmindedly.

"She who hunts," he said flatly. His tone was dead; his face held a blankness I hadn't seen before, something there, something in his face.

It held a far away look that left me with chills. I wasn't sure but for a moment, just a moment – was that fear in his eyes?

I was shaken from this thought by the sounds of horses and men talking from beyond the clearing. I recognized the speech but not the words: Jonda.

"Tucker not worry, all friends here. No harm, promise."

I nodded to him my understanding but the way he said it made me uncomfortable.

Two men, Jonda, appeared in the clearing, followed a few moments later by three more. Their ease vanished instantly upon seeing me.

The first, the smaller of the two, gave a furtive hand signal to the others and they disappeared into the trees. All sounds stopped, no voices, no sounds from the horses, nothing. It was as if they all simply vanished, except the two standing in the clearing.

"This Bowen. Enon friend," he said, placing a heavy hand on the shoulder of the smaller one.

The man made no movement, no smile of acknowledgment. He just stared at me.

I had seen his face in the flash of memories that now seemed little more than a nightmare.

Saved from drowning as a youth by Enon, he had been his one and only steadfast friend, the only true harbor of acceptance in Enon's life.

"This Tucker," Enon started.

"He's cowan," Bowen said with some distaste.

"Tucker Soul bearer for Enon." He grinned.

"This puny man? This... this... cowan?" Bowen asked and walked in a slow circle around me.

"Small yes. Very brave, save Enon's life. Five men all want kill Enon. We fight, Enon, dog, Tucker. Fight like demons. Tucker throws self on knife, save Enon, blood everywhere. Tucker say, 'Only stab once? Tucker brother to Jonda, not hurt Tucker, stab again, give chance run away.' Men shake with fear, give Enon chance to fight each, defeat all.

Tucker want stay, buy ale for Enon, tell stories. Enon say no, not good lose so much blood, come, Enon know medicine woman fix soon. Tucker say 'Why go? Only stabbed once, want fight more.' All unconscious. No one left to fight. So Tucker come.

"Daneba come see Tucker, almost faint so much blood. Enon see again, feel head swim like in deep water, so much blood. Enon scared like little girl for Tucker. Daneba say, 'Brave friend to Jonda. You Soul bearer for Enon now.'

"Tucker say, 'Only one soul? Can hold all Kindred if need, have only ask.'"

Bowen and his companion laughed out loud. They spoke in native tongue to each other for a moment.

Bowen mimicked an animal noise and the others came out of hiding. They numbered fifteen all toll.

I sat down as Enon began all over again for the benefit of those not present for the first telling. This time around, he spoke only in Jonda and made exaggerated faces as he acted out all the parts. They laughed at his antics and several pointed at me, wiping the tears from their eyes. I had to admit he could be funny, even at my own expense.

Bowen was the first to approach me after the telling. He held out his hand to me, accompanied with a large smile.

"The Kindred always has room for one more. Welcome, Brother," he said.

I reached out to shake his hand.

He broke out laughing, as did many of the others.

"Your people are truly strange, Brother. You are Jonda now. Be proud," He thumped his chest with his fist as he spoke. "Holding hands is a woman's greeting, this is the way of men," he said, grabbing my forearm and squeezing firmly.

I was compelled to grip his in return.

Each man came to greet me in this manner, all save one. He was a large man with dark expressions on his face and no love for me. He stood directly before me and spit on the ground at my feet. His angry words, all in Jonda, swept over me.

Enon grabbed the man by the shoulder and spun him around to face him. They began to argue loudly, shoving one another.

"What are they arguing about?" I asked.

"Spath says you are not equal to Jonda. To him you are still cowan. Enon says you are to be treated as an equal. You saved his life and should have the respect the law demands," Bowen explained.

The men formed a circle about them, as their argument became louder, the pushing more intense. Spath's word's rushed out of him in angry torrents, his arms waving wildly. It escalated madly, and then suddenly, as it reached its peak, he pointed toward me and it stopped. They stood silently, chests heaving with the desire to fight. Slowly, Spath lowered his arm. He turned slightly toward me and spit on the ground again.

"What did he say?" I asked.

"He said as long as Noget is here, you are cowan, not Jonda," he said with disappointment.

"Who the hell is Noget?" I asked as something brushed against my leg. To my right, as I looked down Enon's dog was looking up to me. No one said a word. They just stood there, looking at me. "Who the hell is Noget?" I asked again.

Without a word, the circle broke up and began to disassemble.

I stood there alone for a moment, watching the sudden activity.

"Noget," Bowen said softly, lifting his chin toward the dog.

"The dog?" I asked, irritated.

"It is not for me to say, Brother. He will tell you when he is ready."

"Tell me what? Something about the dog? What about the dog?"

"It is not mine to say."

"The dog? Is Noget?" I asked, staring into those cold

canine eyes. Neither the dog nor I gave an inch. I thought for a moment he was in my mind again but the feel was different.

"Dog Noget. Tucker call him dog. We leave now," Enon said harshly, still angry.

The dog snorted, pushing against me lightly and disappeared into the woods. No one spoke. No one looked in my direction. The Jonda, all of whom had been carefree moments before, now behaved as if they believed some hidden truth in Spath's words.

Chapter 5

The trees had grown closer together their shade deepened and travel between them more difficult. I trotted next to Enon. His stride, an easy gate for him, was so enormous I had to make every effort to keep up.

At long last, Enon stopped at the edge of a small opening in the trees. He held his hand over his head and gestured silently.

I had been so busy keeping up with him, I hadn't noticed the others had spread out to the point they were no longer visible, all except Bowen and Enon himself. He gestured for my silence as a light breeze filtered through the trees. I settled onto the ground next to Bowen and waited, happy for the lull.

With a faint rustle of leaves he and the dog trotted away from us. The sound of a strange voice drifted from a short distance away.

Someone was talking to the dog. I sank lower, trying to burrow under the leaves at the base of a large tree. Bowen moved closer to me, hiding me with his body. I wanted to look and edged my way up to peek over his shoulder.

There, not more than fifty feet away, was a half-naked man. He was shorter than a Jonda but larger than me. From the back of his head, grew a long tuft of black hair, braided with leather its full length. His head was shaved with this lone exception. It lay as a single entity across his back, cut square at the bottom of his hunched shoulders. He turned briefly toward us, I was shocked. His face was a dull, ruddy red and stood as stark contrast to the gray tone that covered the remainder of his body. Square, primitive, with a single brow and a protruding jaw his face was like no other I have ever seen. His body and arms were as muscled as any Jonda, only squatter, more compact, and standing on short powerful legs. He was covered only by a loincloth laced at the hip. It seemed unnatural he would be wearing anything at all.

In his right hand, he held a bent stick. He waved it at the

dog and grunted as if to frighten it away. Lifting his head high, he sniffed at the air and turned slowly.

"Norha. Where there is one, there are three," Bowen whispered.

We sat motionless for what seemed like forever, watching the creature with the stick. The dog made a wide circle around him, no bark, and no sound. The man refused to make eye contact with it, pretending it wasn't there.

He kicked at the dirt, searching for what? At last, he bent to pick something up. He held it in a clenched fist over his head and howled. From about his waist he took an object, tied to a piece of sinew. As he spun it, a deep, low throng, something akin to a roar arose, filling the air.

"Roar of the Bear," Bowen whispered, nodding toward the man and his signal.

We sank lower into our hiding. Just as he had predicted two more of the Norha appeared from the trees. They sniffed at the air just as the first had done and turned suspiciously. Satisfied, they inspected his find. He held out his hand to them as they spoke in low grunting tones to one another. I didn't understand their language but apparently Bowen could. His body stiffened.

I tried to divide my attention between the three and the look now spread over his face. He pressed his hand to my shoulder, pushing me lower, indicating I should stay hidden.

"Each is blaming the other, they're looking for Elizabeth," he whispered, getting up.

Something was moving toward me through the underbrush. I held my breath and pushed as low as I could. It was Enon's dog Noget.

He snuffled his way to me and leaned against me, protecting me with his body just as Bowen had before disappearing into the trees.

The voices of the Norha grew louder; rivaling the crunching of leafs under their feet. They were coming closer, following the path of their discovery, and I feared it led to me. They were just on the other side of my tree. The dog pushed hard against me as they started around.

Suddenly, the sound of someone running came from the opposite side of the clearing, and then an unmistakable voice.

"Enon!" it called, shrill, and heart wrenching. Elizabeth.

The Norha clamored in pursuit of the child.

I pushed the dog away and bolted to my feet just as Enon scooped her up in one huge arm and disappeared into the trees.

The angry cries of the Norha rent the air as they gave chase. The dog raced in their direction and I was quick to follow. I did not, however, get very far. Bowen grabbed me, covering my mouth.

"Wait, watch," he whispered.

Enon had disappeared and the Norha were about to do the same. I wanted to help. I struggled to free myself from his grip, but he was much too strong.

"There," he said softly, pointing in the direction the dog had gone. Three more of the Norha appeared to follow the first and then another set and another. Shortly, the forest was alive with them. There had to be more than fifty. Bowen translated as they yelled to one another in their search for Enon.

"We have to help him," I hissed.

"Not yet. There are too many. We can't help Enon if we are captives ourselves."

He was right, of course, but my heart raced with fear, with hate, and a touch of panic.

The voices grew louder and more frantic.

I had come to know those voices; their language was harsh, almost like barking. Then Noget growled; it sounded almost human. The den of an escalating fight was followed by the muffled screams of Elizabeth. My heart jumped into my throat, as the noises became fiercer, more intense.

The sound of the dog was mixed with Enon's voice. They were giving someone, or several someone's, a good piece of hell. My mind raced with the excitement of new voices... Jonda voices.

"They know we are here. My brothers will end this."

The battle split into two directions. The voices turned wild and then, suddenly, silence. We waited.

Nothing, not Norha, not Jonda.

A moment before, the world swirled with anger and the fighting of giant men and at the center of this chaos, the screams of a small child.

The next few minutes passed slowly. Eventually, several

Jonda appeared at the far edge of our sight. They spoke to Bowen, silently with hand gestures and then vanished into the trees once more.

"They have him. There are others looking for us and for the girl. We are not safe here."

"We have to help," I insisted.

"They search for the girl in one direction and take Enon in another. We follow Enon."

"What about Elizabeth?" I asked, torn between the desire to save them both.

"My brothers follow her. They will bring her to safety. Quickly, before we lose them," he said, pulling at my shoulder.

I hesitated for a moment. Four of the Jonda reappeared from the woods to lead us in the direction they had taken Enon, Spath among them. We ran through the trees single file, following the path the dog forged for us. We hoped it would eventually lead us to Enon. The dog ran with purpose, with direction, as if it knew where Enon had gone. It held the lead with Bowen close behind and then the others with Spath bringing up the rear, and I barely in front of him. He pushed at me to hold the pace as I slowed.

"Move, Cowan, I will not lose the truth-sayer because of you," he said, shoving me repeatedly in front of him.

I had not breath left to answer, no strength to do anything other than his bidding, struggling to stay in front of him.

Our trail moved steadily up hill, becoming littered with larger and larger stones and fewer and fewer trees. It was growing dark, making it more difficult to traverse.

I couldn't pull my mind away from the images that the sounds of battle had created. I prayed Enon was still alive. I hoped I could... My thought was broken by yet another shove from Spath. It forced me to the ground. The others stopped and gave me sour looks as they crouched low, waiting for me to gather myself. I got up and moved to the front of the line. The dog was nowhere to be seen and the darkness hung like a suffocating veil.

I wanted to run, just run, but I had no idea where to go. I was lost. I stood there, in the dark, as each took their original position and we were on the move once more.

Eventually, the trees fell away altogether. The ground

rumbled from deep inside. Menacing gurgling sounds surged up from below us. The soil had become black and the rocks huge, sharp and jagged. The air smelled foul, heavy with sulfur. The world had gone mad; no tree, no bush, no blade of grass grew in this wasteland. The dirt had become sand, shifting soft under our feet, lodging itself into every nook and cranny.

The trail of the Norha appeared briefly; only to disappear again as the landscape migrated between the black sand and jagged stone and back to sand again. The trail wandered to the lower right as we slowly moved higher and to the left.

The dog had returned, rushing to the head of the line.

We found ourselves on the edge of a precipice. Below us, a large basin, half a tillage across, encircled by broken stone walls, dropped to a grand depth. At the bottom, the black sand lay smooth and undisturbed, save for a large rock out cropping. Steam punctured the air, carrying the appalling stench, even to our height. Tormented by the groans from deep inside the world, a large, greenish pool foamed and bubbled against the craggy shore of the far side.

An entrance to this netherworld, hidden by its steep walls, became apparent as three of the Norha came into view.

Cautiously, they moved to the center of the basin. They turned slowly, testing the air for danger. Satisfied, one of them howled like a dog and three more came out of hiding to move across the deep sand to the pool's edge.

All six continued to sniff the air, turning as if expecting to find something at any moment. Another howl beckoned and a horde. Hundreds, or perhaps more, Norha poured into the basin. Several of them immediately ran to the outcropping and began to drive iron stakes deep into the stone. The rattle of chains filled the air, sending a shiver up my spine.

In the center of the Norha throng, were three of the Jonda. They struggled against their restraints without avail, only to be beaten, dragged and chained to the stone.

"Enon," Bowen whispered.

My heart pounded in my throat as the angry shouts of the Norha filled my ears. I watched in horror as the horde of Norha beat them with sticks. The chains rattled eerily as they struggled to defend themselves. The Jonda refused to bow to their tormentors, taking all there was to bear.

The dog paced restlessly back and forth, a reflection of Enon's pain.

Bowen spoke harshly in Jonda to the animal, holding it in check.

Suddenly, the Norha fell silent. I pushed closer to the edge, fearing that Enon and his fellows were now dead.

The Norha moved away from the center of the basin, pushing themselves together in small groups. An uneasy silence gripped us all. Something was happening.

They edged warily backwards. Three Norha, slightly larger than the others, marched forward from the unseen opening in the stone wall. Even with no more clothing than the others, they looked different, moved different, more Jonda-like in their manner. Behind them, a woman with red hair kept pace. Shorter by a head, she was well built, muscular in a feminine way. Three more of the larger Norha walked guard behind her.

"Kathryn, She who hunts," Bowen whispered his voice weak and downcast. He collapsed to the ground, turning his back to the basin.

My mind reeled with the memory of Daneba's words, of her warning. With the whole world filled with horrible danger, this woman, this Kathryn was the focus of her concern. From the way the Norha cowered in her presence, the concern was very real.

She stood before Enon and the others.

"We must go before it's too late," Bowen said, rising to his feet.

"What are you talking about? We have to do something to help him." With a flash of memory not my own, I was filled with the thought 'you owe me' and then it was gone as quickly as it came. More of Enon had become me than I had thought.

"He is lost to us now, Brother," he said weakly.

I couldn't form words, couldn't think straight. We had to do something, anything.

"Where is she?" Kathryn's voice, clear, strong and controlled, reached our perch. She held the face of the Jonda closest to her. Chained to the rock, unable to escape, he said nothing.

"And how about you? Where is she?" she asked, moving

to the second. He pulled away from her as well. "And you?" She asked Enon, who didn't acknowledge her at all. She glanced at the Norha and then to the gurgling pool.

Two of them immediately ran to the water's edge to scoop up a cup of the seething fluid.

As the liquid touched the hand of the first, he began to scream in horrible pain. It wasn't water at all, but a lake of acid. The screams were so ghastly, that my heart went out to this lesser being, writhing in pain. He handed the cup to the second, who promptly wiped it clean. His anguish was far less than his companion's but openly present. He, in turn, handed it to Kathryn. She toyed with it, tipping it from side to side for a moment and then moved to Enon.

"I know you," she said, giving him a firm kick in the chest.

He struggled angrily against the chains.

Noget instantly lunged toward the path, rushing to his master's aid. Bowen grabbed the dog in a headlock, wrapping his legs around its body. He tried desperately to wrestle him to the ground.

In less than a heartbeat, the dog stood on all fours, lifting him as if he were but a doll. Two more of the Jonda jumped on the dog, driving him to the ground.

Again, he struggled to his feet, lifting the weight of all three, fighting wildly to free himself. A fourth threw himself on the pile, forcing all to the ground once more. My heart pounded for fear that the scuffle would be heard below.

Thunder at that moment quailed that concern.

"I'll ask only once more... where... is... she... ?" Kathryn asked as she poured several large dollops onto Enon's back. He screamed in tormented pain.

At that instant, the dog cried out, matching the cries of his master. I too felt his anguish in some small part. My shoulder burned with the agony he and the dog were enduring. They surely carried the bulk of the pain, but my share of it was almost unbearable. Slowly, the pain subsided and Spath released me, and I slumped to the ground. The others untangled themselves, releasing the dog. Bowen yanked hard at the skin on the back of its neck, pulling the dog off his feet. Standing on its hind legs it was nearly as tall as Bowen himself.

"Bite him," he ordered in hushed tones, looking at me.

"What?" I asked, bewildered.

"You are Enon's Soul Bearer. Only you can control him. You must prove you are master before he exposes us. Now bite him," he said, thrusting the dog's ear in my direction.

I stood, not certain if he was serious.

"Are you master or not?" he asked as the dog struggled to free itself.

Reluctantly I approached the dog, taking its ear into my mouth and bit down - hard. The dog yelped pulling free of Bowen. I wiped a trickle of blood from my lips. The dog did as it was told.

"Build a fire," Kathryn shouted, and the Norha scrambled to do her bidding. The smoke from the fire rose briskly and then was quickly extinguished. A signal, it could be nothing less.

"They're coming. We must go. We cannot help him now," Bowen said, placing his hand on my shoulder and pointed over the edge.

"Who? Who's coming?" I demanded, but was only given silence for an answer.

The howls of the Norha suddenly reached a new level of excitement.

"Them," he whispered.

As I looked over the edge, I saw that two creatures had entered the basin. The sight of them sent chills up my spine. Apparently, the Jonda chained to the rock with Enon recognized them as well and yanked wildly at their confines.

"What are they?" I asked with loathing heavy in my voice.

"They are us," Spath answered dully.

His words poured over me like cold water. He was afraid and that fear washed over me, soaking me to the bone.

Chapter 6

"Where is she?" Kathryn yelled again, clenching her fist.
There was no answer.

"I see," she said, smoothing her hair. She gave Enon one last kick before turning her attention to the other two. Her voice rose louder and louder in an incantation.

The Norha, even her larger bodyguards, pulled farther back, stepping well behind her. Her voice became more and more harsh.

Clouds overtook the sky, following her behest. Thunder rolled over the landscape, filling our ears with its noise and our hearts with dread. She called to it and it answered. Lightning sprang from the clouds, striking ever closer to our companions, and Kathryn's voice ever more mad with her spell. The ground shook with increasing regularity and strengthening vengeance.

My heart hammered in my ears, but I couldn't turn away. Lightning pounded into the ground, coming closer and closer to her. She was calling it to join with her and not just the lightning – the two creatures were being pulled by her will as well.

They were well over nine feet tall, with horrible fangs, and held an ethereal appearance. They oozed constantly between solid flesh and blood to nothing more than smoke and back again. They hovered just above the ground, with no legs, nor feet to support them. Their skin, a dull blue, was torn in rotten patches. They appeared more dead than alive, ghosts, of a sort, a horrible sight by any measure. Their eyes, even from this distance, glowed a bright yellow. They hovered near Kathryn, shifting in unison to the Norha's unruly chanting.

"Now, my friends, now!" she screamed and the creatures surged forward, entering her body, forging their essence to hers. Her eyes glowed yellow with their presence within her. With their energy added to hers, Kathryn turned her conjuring to the Jonda.

A split second later, lightning struck her full in the chest.

She reeled under its power and screamed like a demon set newly free from hell. The lightning coursed through her and then leaped from her outstretched hand to the first Jonda.

He writhed and screamed in horrible pain. His body contorted, changed, rippling as if something inside of him was fighting to get out. He strained against his chains like a wild animal. Would the screams never stop? Surely they were the worst a man could possibly be forced to endure. I was wrong.

The Jonda's body was being torn apart from within, until he slowly slumped to the ground, a crumpled heap, dead. For a moment there was silence, a dreadful silence that soaked deep into my bones.

Then his body began to jerk of its own volition. It twitched frantically until whatever was inside freed itself. Ripped from his corpse, two entities, one a dull blue and the other a pale white began to swirl over the body. They were unformed, little more than phantoms, each attempting to devour the other. They ripped and tore at each other with increasing speed and savagery.

"What are they?" I gasped.

"Soul Walkers," Bowen said softly, turning to me. "Every man holds within him good and evil. These apparitions are that part of his soul. They are the thread tied to every Jonda. If a Jonda dies alone, this is his fate, unless he gives his life to save another."

"What can we do? How do we stop this?" I insisted.

"There is nothing to be done. It is always the same. They are lost to us," he answered.

I returned my attention to the basin and the clash surging to a conclusion below. The sounds these creatures generated came straight from hell itself. I was transfixed.

"Where is she?" Kathryn screamed at Enon, her voice piercing the terrible sounds.

Again, no answer.

The creatures battled with increasing barbarism, tearing larger and larger pieces from each other. This grotesque dance spun and swirled in widening circles, diving to the ground and then streaming to the sky. Each began to take on a more recognizable form as they gorged themselves with pieces from the other.

Again and again the exchange of ethereal flesh flashed between them. As the tug of war pressed on, it became clear that only the blue creature would survive. It was growing larger and stronger with each new attack. A last howl of anguish from the weaker creature split the air and the victor eagerly swallowed its captive. The creature, now mostly in tatters, pulled itself up to become fully formed, identical to the first two. It hovered in the air for a moment and then slammed into Kathryn adding his essence to hers. She braced for a moment, rocked by the new contact and added depravity.

"Where is she?" she asked, pointing at the Jonda beside Enon.

He stared deep into her eyes before spitting on the ground at her feet. Instantly in response, lightning reached down, striking him directly in the chest and the gruesome ballet began again.

"I can't look," I said, collapsing to the ground. I closed my eyes and covered my ears; I couldn't endure hearing it all over again. It didn't help.

The dog jostled against me. When I opened my eyes, Bowen and the others had crouched close together, passing a knife between them, mumbling a prayer. Each in turn allowed the tip of the knife to touch his forehead and then kissed the blade. It went full circle in this manner as they prayed in unison. One of them produced a silver bowl and then the knife started the circle again. This time, each deliberately made a cut in his left forearm, allowing the blood to rush into the bowl.

"What are you doing?" I asked in a distraught whisper.

"Saving those who we can, Cowan," Spath said with some measure of irritability.

Something inside me pushed to add my blood to theirs. In a trance of personal disbelief, I held my arm out to be cut. It was what Enon would have done. The four of them looked at me, then at each other.

"Not you, Brother," Bowen said with a soft smile.

Spath and one of the other men left the circle for a moment and then returned with a broken branch and a handful of twigs.

"Clean this," Spath said, thrusting the branch at me.

"Your courage did not go unnoticed," Bowen said softly with satisfaction.

I tried desperately to ignore the screams of the Soul Walker and the chanting of the Norha. I did as Spath asked. Each man dipped his knife into the blood and whittled at the twigs. I pulled at the stubble on the branch, unaware of why they wanted me to do it.

"How will this save anyone?" I protested.

"This is a crow," Bowen said, holding one of the twigs out to me. He had already stripped the bark from it, revealing the clean white wood underneath. "These are its wings," he said, holding up two broken feathers and tied them to the stick. "This is the tree of life," he said, pulling the larger branch from my grip. "This is the line that ties all Jonda together, making us the Kindred," he continued, producing a long piece of string and tying it to one end of the stick. "This end is the root of the tree, binding us to the world." He pulled the string tight, flexing the stick. "This end is Bliss, where all Jonda souls go. Today they are carried there on the wings of the crow." He dipped the sharp end of the stick in the blood that swirled at the bottom of the silver bowl and laid it upon the string.

Below us, the sounds of the Soul Walker's screams had stopped, its creation complete. It hovered just beyond Kathryn, eagerly awaiting her command.

Again, she approached Enon. He struggled, yanking frantically against his chains.

"You know what I can do. Where is she?" she screamed.

He gave no answer.

The lightning dove into the ground, inching closer to him with each new strike. The lifeless bodies of his friends lay at his feet as he grappled with the chains, trying to free himself.

"Where is she?" Kathryn shrieked, and the Soul Walker oozed eagerly closer.

Again, no answer came.

Anger and frustration overtook her. Her hand stretched out toward him and the lightning coursed through her. An audible snap of energy split the air as it left her hand and anchored itself in Enon's chest.

"Cayra," he roared, straining to free himself. The chain

attached to his right hand pulled free of its stone mooring and whistled as it cut through the air. The Norha rushed forward as did the Soul Walker. Those too close instantly became its prey and were devoured in torrents of agony.

In a frenzy of Norha blood and death, the Soul Walker charged toward him.

The chain Enon wielded reached out, missing Kathryn by no more than a single link. Several of the Norha closest to him didn't fare as well.

Bowen, watching from our hiding place, jumped to his feet and stretched the string tight to his shoulder. The "crow" took flight with shocking swiftness. It sped to its target with unerring accuracy, driving itself deep into the tattered chest of the Soul Walker.

It bellowed in anguish, falling to the ground, thrashing wildly. The white phantom on which it earlier gorged itself ripped through the opening made by the 'crow', freeing itself. The two battled again, exchanging pieces of each other before the white devoured the blue. In this state, it swirled briefly around Enon and then poured itself into his chest and then was gone.

In that moment, spawned by Kathryn's bidding, lightning drove itself into Enon.

The three Soul Walkers absorbed by Kathryn's body rematerialized and hovered close to Enon. He supported himself on hands and knees gasping for air.

"Cayra," Bowen whispered low and a second "crow" sprang into the air. It whistled, a high pitch whistle, followed by a sickening thud. The creature fell instantly to the ground and was devoured by its white counterpart. The two original Soul Walkers fell upon it, ripping it into small pieces only to have it reassemble and tear in turn at them.

The Norha rushed to the hidden opening and to the trail that lay beyond. They were coming for us. The dog knew it as well and lunged down the trail to meet their advance.

"Stop," I yelled at the dog and all motion in the basin stopped.

"What are you doing? Now they know we are here," Spath said, grabbing my arm.

"They already know we're here."

"They didn't know it was we, only that someone killed

their monster. You are a coward and a liar, Cowan," Spath spit angrily, turning me to face him.

"Yes, sir, I am, and I can do it very well. Now let me do it." I turned to face the basin again. "I am on the King's business. I have the girl, and that man is my prisoner," I yelled at the top of my voice. "Release him. He is in my custody."

"He's trying to save his own skin," Spath protested to the others.

"I'm going to save us all, including Enon," I said firmly.

All five men stood and looked at me, uncertain of my loyalties. After what seemed like forever, Bowen smiled broadly.

"He is a good liar. Go find the others. I will stay," he said.

"I will stay also. If he lies the wrong lie, it will be his last," Spath threatened.

"Fine, just remember, I'm the one talking. No one else. Got it? Too many cooks and all, no one speaks," I said firmly.

They looked confused but nodded their agreement.

The other three disappeared back along the path, splitting up in hopes of finding our deliverance somewhere among the trees.

We began our descent down the trail to the basin. The sound of the Norha rushing toward us overrode the pounding of my heart.

The dog stopped in the middle of the path. It bristled with the sounds from below. I put my hand on his head. I had to handle this just right, or we would all be dead. My mind raced with all the things I was going to say, all the things she might say in response.

My chain of thought was broken, the Norha were there. They walked a wide circle around us, muttering fearfully among themselves. The dog moved to stand in front of me. Its head low, shoulders hunched and teeth bared. Bowen and Spath pressed their backs to mine.

The Norha increased in numbers, forming ring on top of ring around us.

The tension was rising with each passing moment.

"Come along. Take us to your Mistress," I said firmly, without looking any one man square in the face. I marched forward. Mine were the only footsteps.

"Gentleman, if you please," I scolded after a few steps, pointing at the ground directly behind me. It took Bowen and Spath a moment to understand my meaning before they scampered into a servant's position and we started down the trail.

The Norha stood, bewildered as we struck out in front of them. The dog charged forward to trot by my side. Its huge head swung from side to side, glaring at any who braved the path ahead of us. Shortly, as we passed, the Norha fell silently in line.

We were a sight, the dog, me and my Jonda friends and a colossal line of Norha, snaking our way to the bottom of the great basin and to Kathryn. One lie or ten... I prayed I had not taken us from the frying pan into the fire.

Chapter 7

At the bottom of the basin, our procession paused at a sizable opening in the rock face. More of a tunnel than a crevice, its walls were surprisingly smooth as if something hot enough to melt the rock had poured itself through this opening. To the right of the passage, the ground fell away into a deep canyon. A dozen of the Norha ran ahead to announce our arrival.

A hundred feet within the tunnel, the ground rumbled, a deep, low sound, as if to warn us of entering uninvited.

My mind raced wildly as the light filtered in from the opposite side.

The Norha ran in larger and larger numbers past my companions, rushing through the mouth of the tunnel to the light that lay beyond. The basin appeared huge. The gurgling of the lake filled me with dread and the air with more of its noxious fumes.

The smell, potent while we observed from above, was now overpowering, clinging to every fiber of my skin and clothes. My eyes burned with the stench of it.

As we entered, Kathryn turned in acknowledgment and the three larger Norha approached. They stood, shoulders pulled back, defiant of our presence. Their attention was focused almost solely upon Bowen and Spath.

I pushed between them, heading straight for Enon.

"I see you have taken every precaution. That's good. He's a very dangerous man. Are you all right?" I said, pulling hard on his chains.

Kathryn's red hair flowed over her shoulders, framing her very pleasing face. She was slightly taller than I was and very comely. Her green eyes burned with wildness, a passion. The way she held herself spoke volumes of her authority and her desire to be in control. Her clothes clung tightly to her body, every curve a tribute to desire.

I had met this type of woman only once before, and that was just for a few brief moments. She could have asked for anything and I would have most likely done everything to please her, had I not seen all that had taken place before.

I wouldn't have thought it possible of her.

"Yes," she answered suspiciously.

"Good, I didn't see it myself but my man here said you were under attack and managed to kill it before it could harm you."

"Yes, thank you," she said slowly.

I looked at Enon to break the thoughts coursing through my mind. His eyes met mine and I followed them to the dog. It had stopped in front of Kathryn. My mind raced, I was so concerned about what the Jonda's might say, I didn't even think about the dog. It sat right in front of her, staring, ears flat against its head.

"Is this yours?" She asked, waving a hand to dismiss the dog.

"Yes," I said. I glanced quickly at Enon. I called to the dog.

It broke its glance long enough to acknowledge me.

"Come," I commanded.

It returned its glare to Kathryn.

"Come," I repeated angrily.

Slowly, reluctantly, it came and sat by my side. It swung its attention to Enon for a moment and then back to me.

"It doesn't look like your dog," she said, moving closer.

"He is a new acquisition. Now then, please tell me how much you will need for your trouble and I will see to it the King's gratitude is in your hands within two days."

She was visibly stunned, unable to respond.

"Take him into custody," I ordered, but Bowen and Spath stood confused, motionless. I had to do something. We were in trouble.

"Now," I yelled and reached out to the one closest to me and slapped him as hard as I could. It was Spath.

The smack shocked Kathryn. Its sound made the Norha flinch involuntarily and take a step back.

"Yes, sir. Sorry, sir," Bowen said, realizing my deception first. He grabbed Spath's arm to control his reaction. Surely, if looks could kill, my death resided in Spath's face. Bowen yanked hard on his arm again, pulling him toward Enon.

"Sorry, sir," Spath said, turning his angry eyes to the ground.

"I'm sorry you had to see that. It's the only thing they understand," I said apologetically to Kathryn.

"That was a brave thing to do, Citizen," she said with a little admiration in her voice.

"Not at all, they are only Jonda, little more than overgrown children," I said, but my heart sank with the words. They were a brave, wonderful race of people and I hated hearing those words come from my mouth.

Even with their backs turned, it was obvious Bowen and Spath did as well. They grappled with the chains holding Enon, cutting at the leather strapped to his wrist.

"The child, Citizen, you said you have her?" Her body shifted slightly closer.

"Oh that. Yes, I've already sent her along with Chancellor Grimwell and a hundred of the Kings guard; she'll be fine. Now about your reward," I said as smoothly as I could.

She twitched visibly at my words.

"Chancellor Grimwell?" She repeated. Her voice held an edge of irritation.

"Yes, the King's personal adviser. He's meeting Governess Eloise who will return the child to the King personally. Lovely people really. Do you know them?"

She shifted her weight again, away from me this time. I had hit a nerve.

"No, I don't know them," she mouthed weakly. It was clear something heavy ate at her mind.

"More's the pity. Delightful people. I'm sure you would find them most charming. If you could give me some idea, the reward, for your efforts I will send them along with the Chancellor," I said, glancing to Bowen who still struggled with Enon's confines.

Several Norha ran to us, returning from the outside world.

Their leader approached Kathryn to whisper in her ear. She turned and walked a few steps away, giving me a very distasteful look.

"Well, it would seem our business is done here," I said, turning to Bowen once more. He smiled, nodding quickly, his signal Enon was freed.

"Who did you say you were?" She asked harshly.

"Tucker, Tucker Littlefield a friend to the King."

"As am I, Citizen, but these are dangerous times and

caution is our watch word," she said, sliding closer to me.

"Agreed," I said with trepidation.

"Perhaps some proof."

"Ah, I see, certainly," I said, and retrieved the letters Governess Eloise had slid into my pocket.

Kathryn opened them slowly, eyeing me closely. She read them slowly, looking for some sign of forgery.

"It would seem the King holds you in high regard," she said with disdain, returning the papers to me.

"Bring him along, gentlemen. The King is waiting," I said, placing the papers in my pocket once more.

"No need, Citizen. I sent my men to find the good Chancellor. They tell me he's on his way here now." A wicked smile slowly crossed her lips.

"Really? How very thoughtful of you, Mistress Kathryn, but I assure you we can find him ourselves,"

"Not at all, Citizen. I can hardly wait to meet the gentleman. I insist that you stay. Our good Chancellor will be here shortly." Her words flowed smoothly out of her mouth, as if she knew something we didn't.

"That won't be necessary," I started.

"I insist," she said firmly.

"With my thanks," I said with a slight bow. I had to think of something. We had come this far, too far to give up now.

"They will have to be tied, for the night, for security," she said, pointing at Bowen and Spath. She uttered the words softly, touching my shoulder as she spoke.

I looked about, trying to think of something, anything, for my next move.

"How many men do you have here? Fifty? Sixty? More?" I took a few steps away, eyeing the men along the basin walls. I needed to pull away from the warmth of her hand.

"More than four hundred, Citizen, and more on the way," she said with pride.

"Only four hundred? Then I understand your insecurity. Please accept my apologies. I had no idea your men were so frightened by Jonda. After all, there are two of them and a third, but he doesn't really count, does he? What with his hands tied and all."

A grumble of Norha voices swirled angrily through the basin, just the reaction I was hoping for.

"See what you've done?" I said, turning to Bowen and slapping him playfully on the shoulder. "You should be ashamed of yourself. You've frightened them."

Again the Norha voices rose, louder, more angry than before. Their grunting and shouting became harsher. They beat their chest and ventured closer to us.

"Hold," Kathryn yelled, holding up her hand to stop their advance.

They froze in place and yelled louder still.

"You are a curious little man. Did you know the Norha are the most feared, most vicious tribe in the world? They almost wiped out the Jonda single handedly. Did you know they often eat those they defeat in battle?" she whispered to me as she walked a slow circle around me, smoothing her hand across my shoulders.

"That would account for how ugly they are, but not for why four hundred of them tremble like little girls in the presence of two good Jondas," I said. At this point I had nothing to lose.

"Shortly, Citizen, we will see, who is afraid of whom," she said, pulling her hand from my shoulder. She turned to walk away, giving her hips an extra swing.

I watched those hips intently. With each step she took away, the Norha stepped closer.

"Not good, Tucker want woman bad for Jonda," Enon teased, pulling himself to his full height, rubbing his wrist. There was no need of pretense anymore.

"Not me. Just looking, that's all. Might not get a second chance," I said, turning to face him.

"It will be dark soon, Brother. We will need fire and something to eat," Bowen's voice came flat, dry.

I nodded my agreement.

There was a ring of Norha, five men deep, not more than ten feet away. Enon approached the closest and wrenched a torch from his hand.

"Bring food," he ordered.

The Norha stood motionless and soundless.

The air hung still, filled with the stench of the acid lake and of the Norha. Standing this close their smell was strong, a rank, putrid odor, like a dead animal.

The torch sizzled and popped, pulsating with the tension of the moment.

"Decent food for decent men," I chided. I had no desire to eat anyone I might have met in a tavern. No sound, no movement met my affront.

Enon pushed deeper into the rows of men. They muttered angrily to one another but did little to block his advance. Those at the outer ring began to step aside. Slowly, as they separated, an open path between us and the basin's exit appeared.

In little more than whispers, the Norha began to chant and at the edge of the growing darkness, Kathryn emerged, escorting two of the monsters. Her face held an expression of wicked delight as she waved her hand, releasing them in our direction.

The Soul Walkers glided closer as if drawn by the light of the torches and the chanting of the Norha. The sight of their yellow eyes, glowing with the reflection of the torches, made my body jerk. A shiver of fear ran deep within my spine.

"Come, Enon set free," he yelled to the wraiths, thrusting his torch into the air.

The Norha voices rose to a deafening clamor. The creatures slid closer, their fingers flexed in a greedy, menacing manner.

"Yes, come, Enon send to Bliss," he screamed, pounding his chest, waving them closer as the Norha roared their disapproval.

I thought we would be engulfed by the sheer mass of them or devoured alive by the creatures themselves.

The Norha cheered wildly as the monsters inched closer. I stared in disbelief as Bowen slipped a dagger into Enon's hand as he taunted them to come closer still.

And they did. Inch by inch, emanating a low, sick snarl; the sound slid pass their lips in a vile, continuous gurgle and their eyes focused almost solely on Enon.

The Norha stepped back with genuine fear as one of the monsters glided slightly ahead of the other. For a moment it hung motionless save for its fingers, and murmured its hate. It held its head and eyes low. Its fingers moved slower and slower. It was going to charge.

"Come, Goddess waiting, Enon waiting," he yelled angrily, turning Bowen's dagger repeatedly in his hand.

The fiend lunged and the Norha roared wildly. With a blood-chilling scream of hate, it rushed forward, more vapor than solid, more teeth and claw than man. Its eyes burned bright with its evil.

Enon stood poised, ready to receive the force of the blow he knew was coming. As if out of thin air, the dog, all but forgotten, suddenly appeared in front of me.

It threw its body full force into mine, driving me to the ground and knocking the wind out of me. I gasped for breath, horrified.

The clamor of the Norha was drowned in the screams from the creature, now thrashing on the ground next to me. I couldn't move. I couldn't speak.

There, not three feet away, the monster roared in agony, Bowen's dagger lodged deep in its tattered chest.

The life within poured through the hole, becoming the other half of itself. The grotesque ballet had begun again. The horrible sounds penetrated my very soul and I could stand no more. Something deep inside of me called to me to do the unthinkable and I did its bidding.

Bowen's dagger, torn free in the struggle, appeared on the ground next to me as the creatures fought for dominion over the other. As if in a trance, I grabbed the knife and plunged it into the back of the Soul Walker. It screamed with unholy anguish and spun, turning its angry attention to me.

Both Enon and the dog were instantly there, diving upon the creature, becoming entangled with the monstrosity writhing before me. Their entanglement was short-lived. The creatures rolled into the ring of Norha tearing larger and larger pieces from one another, unaware of those around them. They rose to the sky and back again, filling the air with their horrible sounds.

The Norha roared in angry voices and swung their sticks at the pale white entity. It had become apparent, even to them, ultimately it would win.

The monster, or what was left of it, wallowed on the ground, drowning in the gaining strength of the other. A last desperate howl escaped from it as it was devoured in sum total.

The white victor dove at the heads of the Norha, chasing them about before crashing, full force, into Enon's chest. He reeled for a moment from the impact and then pulled himself to full measure.

A blood-chilling scream from the second, forgotten, Soul Walker pierced the air. It charged forward, clearing a path through the Norha for its advance. Revenge burned deep within those yellow eyes. The thing was coming. I rose to stand next to Enon. The dagger burned hot in my hand, my blood running as hot as the dagger.

"Hold," Kathryn's voice yelled over the din.

The Soul Walker stopped its advance as if held by an invisible rope, struggling against the unseen power that gripped it.

"My, we are full of surprises," she said, pushing her way through the Norha. She slid her hand to my shoulder and walked a slow circle around me again.

"Who would have thought? Such a brave little thing. Did you really think you could kill a Walker?" she cooed.

"Why not? He did," I said, pointing at Enon with the dagger. My heart pounded wildly in my chest as I struggled to catch my breath.

"Why not? He did. Oh that's good, Citizen. Why not? He's a Jonda, you imbecile."

"I told you, my dear, we have nothing to fear from this charlatan," a familiar voice said, a man stepping into view.

"Ahh, the venerable Chancellor Grimwell. Why am I not surprised?" I said with disgust.

"Just kill the bastard and be done with it," he hissed.

"In good time, dearest, all in good time let's have a little fun first. We have our friend Mr. Tutelo to consider, not to mention, his guest."

"Enon ready, bring all walking dead. Enon send to Bliss." He pushed his chest out and pressed against Grimwell.

"Kill them now, Kathryn. End this nonsense before... "

"See what you've done, Enon? Now you've frightened the good Chancellor," I chided.

"Brave little thing, isn't he? He thought he could kill a Walker." She beamed with pride. "How about you, Grimwell, think you can take one?"

"This is ridiculous. End this now, Kathryn," he barked.

"Sounds like a no to me," I said.

"Don't you just love him? So bold, so...*unaware*," she said with a surprising level of glee.

"Pity, he's so short," Grimwell sniped, matching my disdain.

"Better than being a coward," Kathryn said, turning her back to him.

She smoothed her hands over my chest, outward over my shoulders before patting them lightly. "Besides, he's not all that short."

"Tell you what. I'll give you the benefit of the doubt, but I'll have to take Chancellor Grimwell here into custody. As I said, I have a letter from the King giving me full authority," I said as firmly as I could.

"Oh, Goddess, he believes it," Grimwell said, rolling his eyes.

"You are priceless, Citizen. Really, I haven't had this much fun in... I don't know how long," she said, wiping tears from her eyes.

"Where Izie?" Enon intoned, grabbing Grimwell by the throat. Straight to the heart of it, I liked that about him.

Grimwell pulled free of his grip and stepped back, rubbing his neck.

"He's right. Where's the child?" I pressed.

"Ah... men, I knew it was too good to last. She's fine, Citizen, you have my word."

"You'll forgive me if I want to see for myself,"

"I am here," a tiny voice, soft, flat, without life, drifted to us from the center of the Norha. A path opened in them and Elizabeth stepped forward.

"Izie," Enon called. Anxiety tinged his voice, the hope, and the love he held for her caused it to crack. It pulled at my heart in ways I cannot describe.

Her eyes where dull and her skin held no life or color. Her arms didn't swing as she walked; no emotion crossed her face.

She looked as lifeless as the Soul Walker that still hung motionless just outside Kathryn's reach.

Enon's body lurched forward in an effort to hold and comfort the child. The Norha would have no part of it.

"Izie," Enon yelled, pushing them aside, knocking several

to the ground. Dozens of them jumped on him to hold him in place.

She made no outward sign of recognition. The child moved to Kathryn's side, staring straight ahead, unaware of her surroundings.

"Monster. What done to Izie?" Enon asked angrily.

"She's fine. Just a little tired," Kathryn said, smoothing her hand over the back of the child's head. A small blue spark of energy crackled softly as it escaped from her ring to Elizabeth.

"Izie," Enon pleaded softly, kneeling in front of her. "Come, Enon take home to mother."

She made no movement, no blink of recognition at his voice or offer. From my position, I could see the spark connecting Kathryn to the child change with Enon's words. It thickened and flexed, spreading like depraved fingers over the back of Elizabeth's skull.

"We have what we want. End this farce," Grimwell barked.

"Yes, I suppose we do," Kathryn said absentmindedly, and the energy fingers grew smaller before disappearing entirely.

Elizabeth's tiny body shook momentarily. Enon scooped her up in his huge arms before she could slip to the ground.

"Pure heart," he whispered and kissed her forehead.

She laid unconscious, limp little more than a wisp of her normal self. He cradled her in one arm and softly stroked her hair as he stood.

"I told you, she's fine," Kathryn said. She reached out to follow his lead and brushed the child's hair.

Enon slapped her hand away and the crowd of Norha flinched.

"Not fine. Monster, not touch, Enon say it so," he spit between clenched teeth.

"She's mine now, Mr. Tutelo. Her future is not your concern," she said with determination, reaching to pull the child from his grasp.

"What are you talking about, Kathryn? She has no future. That was the plan," Grimwell said, turning her forcibly to face him.

"Enon send all to Bliss before turn Izie to monster," he

threatened before kissing the child's forehead again. He nuzzled her ear and for a moment I thought I heard him whisper to her.

"Things change, Grimwell," she said, turning away from him.

"This is madness. Kill them. Kill them all and be done with it," Grimwell ordered, pointing at me.

"You would kill a child? You are a coward," I spat on the ground at his feet.

"You're right, Grimwell. I have all that I want. I don't really need you at all now, do I?" Kathryn said, reaching for Elizabeth again.

Enon stepped back, drawing the child tighter to his chest, avoiding Kathryn's touch.

"You bitch," Grimwell screamed, spinning her around again to slap her face. The air rang with the sound of it.

The Norha swarmed over him, stretching his limbs to their limits, holding him spread eagle.

"You should have known that once I had the girl, I would no longer have need for you," Kathryn said, approaching him slowly.

"You can have the girl. I have all I need. The Jonda is as good as dead. The King is at my bidding and the Kingdom is mine. All mine. Keep the girl. Release me," Grimwell said, struggling to pull free.

"The Kingdom? You always did think too small. The Kingdom means nothing," she chided.

"What the hell are you talking about? You kidnapped Elizabeth so you could dethrone the King?" I asked angrily.

"Grimwell did. I, on the other hand, have a much larger vision of the future.

I knew of his little attempts to insert himself as King, so I offered to help him, in exchange for the child," Kathryn said, turning to speak to me over her shoulder.

"Izie, know truth. Soon nowhere Grimwell hide. Better Izie gone," Enon growled.

"He's right, you know. She has many of the same interesting abilities her father was blessed with," Kathryn said.

"Her father? Who's her father?" I asked, confused.

"Oh, Citizen, you are priceless. How did I ever get along without you?" she laughed.

"Kathryn, you have what you want, release me. I can still be a great deal of help to you. You gain nothing by my death," Grimwell pleaded.

"Enon gain," he said roughly. He shifted his weight as the dog reappeared at his side. It peered at me, blinking briefly, and then turned its back.

"Truth-sayer," Elizabeth whispered weakly, opening her eyes.

"Pure heart," Enon whispered in return. He kissed her forehead tenderly. Slowly, he lowered her to the ground next to the dog. She wobbled on weakened legs as his arm slipped from her. She braced herself against the animal for a moment.

Enon looked into her tiny face and smiled weakly. He drew a deep breath and glanced at me, lifting his chin.

"Now Izie, now," he shouted and lunged at Kathryn, driving her to the ground. The Norha instantly set upon him, screaming and beating him.

Bowen, Spath and I pulled madly at them, trying to help all that we could until we were restrained. Buried under a seemly endless number of Norha, Enon had wrapped his arms around Kathryn and refused to let her go. She screamed incoherently from under him as they fought to free her.

"The child, you idiots, the child," she screamed, finally free, rising to her feet. She thrust out her hand and my eye followed its lead.

Elizabeth, riding on the back of Enon's dog, had almost reached the other side of the basin. The Norha vaulted at Kathryn's command and gave chase.

Lightning sprang from her fingertips, striking the ground close to the dog. Elizabeth clung to the animal with a fierce grip, her tiny legs wrapped around its midsection. It ran with an unnatural speed, straight for some unseen goal. The ground rumbled more fiercely with each new explosion that leaped from Kathryn's hand. Each time, at the last instant, the dog changed course just before the lightning could reach out and halt their escape.

"Elizabeth," a desperate voice called out from the rim of the basin.

"Nanna," Elizabeth's frail voice echoed off the basin walls.

There at its brink, Governess Eloise lay on the ground, her arms outstretched over its rim. Her terrified cry tore at my heart.

The ground roared and shook as if in great pain as Kathryn sent bolt after bolt, coming ever closer to the dog with each new attempt. The lake splashed violently onto the shore, sending rivers of the acid over its edge, cutting deep ruts into the sand.

Lightning exploded with greater savagery, raining dirt and rocks over the entire basin.

"Stop it!" I screamed at Kathryn. "Stop it!"

The Norha beat me as I struggled to get free. Two of the Norha held my wrist high over my head, trying to restrain me. In the struggle my palm was forced open and outward. They froze briefly and then fell to their knees screaming, babbling wildly. The others quickly followed suit.

"Get up, you fools, get up," Kathryn screamed.

Only she, the Jondas and I were left standing. Enon grabbed my wrist, and held it high; turning me so all could see the brand placed there.

"Soul Bearer take all," he yelled and each buried its face deeper into the sand.

"Get up. He has no power. I command you! Get up," Kathryn screamed. She kicked several of the Norha with no avail.

Enon released me to grab her. She kicked, scratched and screamed.

With their arms extended over their heads, the Norha bellowed their protest, beating the ground violently but not one looked up.

"Soul Bearer take all," Enon repeated, bellowing at the top of his voice.

Kathryn fought him with all her might but it bore little effect. Enon pulled her along at his will.

She screamed something and the Norha giving chase stopped in their tracks, all save one. The others were now focused solely on us and were on their way to rescue her.

A deep growl from the forgotten Soul Walker pierced the air. Released from its invisible yoke, it now rushed towards us.

Enon threw Kathryn to the ground and spun to meet its advance.

The dog raced up the basin wall along a narrow ledge, Elizabeth clinging to him for dear life. The animal scaled the steep rampart, higher and higher, leaping from one stone outcropping to another, until it was moments from the top. It struggled frantically to hold its footing as Elizabeth reached for Governess Eloise's outstretched hands.

"Come to me, child," the woman screamed and leaned farther over the side.

At that instant, lightning sprang from Kathryn, reaching out for them. It exploded within inches, sending the dog, Elizabeth and Governess Eloise rolling down the basin wall in a cloud of gray dust.

"Izie!" Enon anguished cry vibrated to the very core of me. He spun as if to run to her and was caught from behind by the Soul Walker and driven to the ground by the blow. Blood ran freely from his shoulder. The creature stood over him and howled with delight, its fingers flexing with greedy hunger.

I grabbed for Enon's knife just as Kathryn did the same. I got it first and received her wrath on the back of my head. I pointed it, first at her and then at the monster as it peered over its shoulder at me. No remnant of kindness, no mark of any Jonda soul held residence there. I couldn't help but shudder as I looked into those unmerciful eyes.

"My life for yours, Brother," Bowen yelled and drove his body into the creature's midsection, bowling it over.

The monster reeled from the attack, immediately rolling to its feet again and braced for the charge. It howled and then lunged for Bowen.

My heart pounded wildly, filling my ears with the rush of my blood for fear and the lack of knowing what to do.

"Cayra," called a voice from the brink of the basin and a "crow" whistled over my right shoulder. I felt the brush of air in its passing as it sought its target. The creature released a tortured scream as the other part of itself poured from the fresh wound. It had begun again.

"I will take all. Do not tempt my patience," I yelled, holding out my palm for the Norha to see. They chanted their protest but remained face down, even those coming to Kathryn's aid. All save one.

He raced toward Elizabeth, shielding his face with his

hands. He made every effort not to look at me.

At first, Elizabeth appeared dead, as did the dog and the Governess. The lone Norha scooped her up and ran. She hung limp over his shoulder, as if her body no longer held bones.

Groggy, weak and disoriented, the dog forced itself to stand just as Enon rose to his feet.

"Izie," Enon cried.

The dog shook its head briefly, then turned just enough to make eye contact with him and was off in pursuit.

Lightning sprang from Kathryn in horrible numbers, striving for the dog. The crash of thunder exploded with furious regularity, lapping one over the other.

The ground rumbled in great pain and began to pitch and roll. The acid lake poured over its confines, opening a deep rift and making the air even more putrid.

Enon turned his weakened body and his anger to Kathryn. He lunged at her, forcing her to the ground once more. Blood was everywhere, covering her clothing as well as his. She screamed and cursed at him. They rolled over each other as well as the Norha.

"Izie, Tucker, Izie!" Enon yelled and the realization of his words jumped into my mind. I turned. The Norha with Elizabeth ran toward the basin entrance, the dog only paces behind.

Bowen and Spath were tangled in the struggle between Kathryn and Enon, trying to pull them apart, to control her.

A massive bolt leapt out from somewhere in that dark sky, striking Enon. All four were thrown clear of the other, unconscious.

"I will take all!" I yelled as many of the Norha began to rise. They buried their faces again with the threat of my voice.

The Governess Eloise stumbled toward me. Her face was dirty and bruised her body weak. I held her in my arms and she leaned her weight into me.

"It will be alright," I whispered, brushing the hair from her face.

"Not yet, Citizen," Kathryn hissed. She pushed at the ground on all fours to steady herself. From the depths of her very soul she gathered the energy to throw one last blinding bolt. It ripped through the air with a deafening roar, reaching out for the dog. Instantly, the basin filled with the creature's mournful cry and it dropped to the ground, dead.

My heart pounded with panic at the sound. I ached at its loss.

Kathryn rose to unsteady feet and called to the Norha carrying Elizabeth.

"Bring the child to me," she ordered hoarsely. She kicked Enon's unconscious body in her passing to greet him.

Driven by the power she unleashed on the dog, the ground undulated and more of the lake poured into the fresh opening, widening its girth. The sharp sizzle of sand washing away dominated. The rift began to stretch farther and farther, sending its eroding fingers in every direction.

The runner approached, laying the child's limp body at Kathryn's feet.

"Elizabeth," Eloise whispered, dropping to the ground to cradle the child in her arms. She ran her hand over Elizabeth's face, wiping away the dirt.

"I've won, Citizen. The child is mine," Kathryn said weakly, her energy spent.

"You monster, you will never take her while I live," Eloise said, pulling the child tighter to her.

"A minor detail, I assure you," she replied coldly.

At that moment, the ground rumbled again and a fracture opened at our feet. The lake poured into it, dissolving deeper and deeper with each passing second. I pulled at Eloise and moved away from the encroaching edge. A gaping fissure sprang to life between Kathryn, the Norha, and us. We on one side and they on the other. It grew in depth and length in the blink of an eye in every direction. At the bottom, acid flowed freely in great torrents. It had become fifteen, perhaps twenty, feet deep and more than twelve feet across, much too wide to jump and too long to go around. We were on an island of safety.

"Throw her to me, Citizen, before it's too late, and I will let you live," Kathryn said, moving to the very edge of the divide.

"You've lost. Take your people and go," I chided.

"I have not come this far to leave without her. Give her to me," she screamed.

"Nanna," Elizabeth cried softly and wrapped her arms around Eloise's neck.

I had hoped Enon would have revived by now, but he had not.

Kathryn barked orders to the Norha and they rose to her command. They grouped themselves in sets of three and ran, trailing off toward the entrance. The sound of their feet pounding in unison suddenly joined with the whirling drone of the bear, flooding the basin with an eerie sound.

Kathryn made no movement as the Norha turned, chanting, heading back straight for us. The chanting increased, becoming faster and faster as they ran. Those at the head of the line rushed to make the jump to our side but fell to the bottom into the acid. Their screams of agony were short lived as the next jumped and landed on top of them, followed by another and yet another. Dozens upon dozens of them threw themselves over the edge and more followed until a bridge of living bodies was created for Kathryn and she simply walked across.

"Give her to me," she said harshly.

"Never," Eloise said, standing, pushing Elizabeth behind her.

"Then die," Kathryn shouted and backhanded the governess across the face, sending her sprawling to the ground.

Elizabeth ran to hide behind me.

"I'm taking her, Citizen," she said with full menace. The air began to crackle as she raised her hand toward me. The lightning was coming.

"Of my own free will," came Elizabeth's tiny voice, barely audible, she stepped out from behind me and walked unafraid to Kathryn. "Leave them alone and I will go with you... of my own free will."

Kathryn slowly lowered her hand, considering the child's words.

"Of your own free will?" she repeated.

The child nodded her agreement.

"I won't allow it." I said, pulling the young girl behind me again. I turned Bowen's dagger over in my hand and prayed Enon would wake up soon.

"Caution, Citizen, caution. You heard the child. She wants to go with me."

"Only to save our lives," I countered. We walked in a slow circle, each waiting for an opportunity to show itself.

"Of my own free will," Elizabeth called. She now stood on the other side of the divide, surrounded by Norha.

I was shocked. My heart pumped madly. I stared in disbelief. She held out her tiny hand toward us. Her face was a sad silhouette of resolution. I had to do something, anything. I couldn't just let her walk away.

Kathryn straightened and walked across the bodies of her minions to take her hand. At her passing the Norha, those that could, rose and followed. The remainder, the broken and the dead, slowly washed away in the stream of acid and the bridge was gone.

"You've lost, Citizen," Kathryn said with a wicked smile.

"Elizabeth!" Eloise cried, rising to her knees, holding her arms out to the child.

"It's alright Nanna. I promise," Elizabeth said weakly.

Time seemed to stop. I heard no sound and saw nothing but the child's face and my heart sank.

"No fear, Pumpkin. Enon come for you," the Jonda said more dead than alive. Enon struggled to stand to look Kathryn in the eye. "And for you," he threatened and then slumped to the ground once more.

"Come, I can always use more Walkers," she chided.

Kathryn turned and disappeared with Elizabeth into the mass of Norha. They marched off toward the entrance and slowly disappeared through its gaping mouth.

We were alone, deserted on an island of rock, helpless as that monster walked away with our 'Izie'.

Only the hiss of dissolving sand was left. No Norha voice, no thunder, no marching. We were alone, stranded on the rock Enon and the others had been chained too. They, more accurately she, had won. Elizabeth was gone.

"Well," Eloise's voice broke the silence. She stood and brushed the dirt from her clothes. "What are you waiting for? Go after them."

Chapter 8

"We can't just sit here," Eloise said impatiently, "they have my baby." She paced restlessly from edge to edge of our new prison.

I wanted to say something but didn't know what. I sat down next to Enon and inspected his wound.

"He'll live," Bowen said, cradling Enon in his arms.

"With little thanks to our cowan," Spath said with his usual distaste.

I didn't say anything. I just nodded and let it go. A long uncomfortable silence hung over us. I closed my eyes, the sound of the sand eroding ever deeper at the bottom of the gorge.

"They'll be here soon," Bowen said softly to Enon.

"Who?" I asked, only half interested. I toyed with the smaller stones strewn around me, tossing them over the edge.

"Our Brothers, they will come." Bowen whispered in my direction.

"Not soon enough for me," Eloise groused. "Do you have to just sit there?" Her darker side had reappeared.

"Where would you like me to sit?" I asked, without stirring.

"I don't want you to sit at all. I want you to bring Elizabeth back to me," she retorted.

"If I could, you know I would," I said. "What are you doing here anyway?" I was hoping to put her on the defensive for a change.

"Looking for you and our Chancellor Grimwell," she said, sitting down next to me, excited to share her personal account of things. "Your horse returned but no word came from Enon. You had either run away or never got there or you killed him. So I came to hunt you down."

"Him? Kill Enon?" Spath asked. He and Bowen repeated several Jonda words to one another and laughed out loud.

"Why would I kill Enon?" I asked annoyed.

Bowen and Spath roared with laughter, slapping each other on the shoulder.

They pointed at me, and then at Enon and laughed all the more.

"Let's just say you ran away," Eloise accused.

"I didn't run away," I protested. "Things got complicated, that's all."

"So I've noticed," she said and scooted closer. "I had prepared a horse to look for you when the good Chancellor came upon me. He convinced me he should come along for my own safety. Then he shamed the King and two dozen of his best into joining us. We, all of us, came to look for you. That was four days ago."

"How did you get here?" I asked.

"Three days ago, Grimwell convinced the King to go on ahead, I would only slow him and his men down," she said and angrily pulled at her tunic to straighten it. "It was only Grimwell and myself. After a few hours of riding in circles he told me to stay put and he would ride ahead to find the King. It didn't take long for me to figure out he wasn't coming back. I followed his tracks as best I could, until I became lost, and then they came along," she said, standing.

I followed her gaze and there on the opposite side, bigger than life, two Jonda trotted in our direction. Bowen and Spath stood to meet their greeting.

They spoke in happy tones to one another, we on our side of the divide and they on the other. As they spoke, Bowen gestured first to Enon and then to the opening. He was explaining how we came to be in this predicament.

Spath nodded and pointed in unison without a word. Bowen pointed limply into the growing darkness, toward where the dog lay. It was agonizing, even in Jonda; the words pulled at me. After a few moments of silence they began to speak rapidly to one another. One of the newcomers turned and trotted off into the darkness.

"Where's he going?" I asked frustrated.

"To get us off this rock," Bowen answered. "He'll be back."

After a long while, as promised, he returned. In his right hand he carried a small limb and over his shoulder a large coil of rope. Throwing it to the ground, he picked up one end and tied it about himself, the other to the limb. He began to swing it over his head, faster and faster in ever widening circles before thrusting it in our direction. The coil hissed as it unwound through the air, punctuated by a dull thud by the limb's landing. Spath grabbed the rope and tied it about his waist as he spoke in his native tongue to Bowen. They nodded in agreement and then, with no warning, he jumped over the side.

"Dear Goddess," Eloise blurted out. Clinging to the rope, Spath swung to the opposite side, crashing feet first into the disintegrating wall.

He spun in mid air briefly before his two companions pulled him to the top and to freedom. Again, the limb was tied to the end of the rope and flung to our side.

"You are next, brother," Bowen said, handing the rope to me.

"Me? What about her?" I asked.

He looked confused, first at me and then sheepishly at Eloise.

"In my village," he said softly, leaning closer to me, "it is customary for the husband to lead, to make all things safe for his wife to follow."

It took me a moment to realize he was talking about Eloise.

"She's not my wife!" I cried, perhaps a little shriller than I would have liked. I was shocked, frozen in place.

"Who just insulted me more? He for thinking me your wife or you for denying it so girlishly?" Eloise asked, glaring at me, her arms folded.

"I only meant..."

"I know what you meant. Now go," she intoned and pointed at the rope.

"I'm going, I'm going," I said. Anything had to be better than that look.

"In my village," Bowen whispered as he tied the rope around me, "the oldest daughter is always married first. Spath fell in love with the youngest, very pretty, a true love. He was told he must wait until the elder sister found her mate. She is not easily pleased, unhappy with her fate and her younger sister's happiness. Time passed too slowly for him and young love is very impatient.

"It is our custom... to make the youngest his wife he must also bring the oldest into his lodging and provide for her until she finds a man."

"I don't understand," I said as he tugged the rope to ensure it was tight.

"For all his days, Spath has two wives, the pleasure and love of one, the hate and loathing of the other, never truly happy, never truly miserable."

"What does all this have to do with me?" I asked.

"That woman," he said, nodding toward Eloise, "makes Spath's life look like a festival. For the balance of your life, she is your wife."

And with that he pushed me over the edge. The rope hung loose for a blink of an eye and then pulled hard at my midsection, squeezing the air out of me. My heart pitched upward to stick in my throat. The other wall loomed large, racing toward me. I spun to meet it. The dull thud of my feet striking the wall shook me to the very core. For a moment, I hung there, spinning slowly in the darkness. Only the sound of the acid dissolving ever deeper and the groan of the rope kept me company. Suddenly, I lurched upward as the rope slide over the upper edge. I swung like a pendulum and then was yanked again, harder this time, followed by another and another, until I reached the top. The two Jonda held the rope as Spath got on one knee to pull me to safety.

"Thanks," I said, struggling to untie the rope.

"I am waiting, Husband," Eloise called out sarcastically.

Spath peered across the abyss before slapping my hands away to untie the rope for me.

"Perhaps, Cowan, it would have been better if I had let you fall," he said, his voice much too serious for me.

"Husband," her voice again, sounding more sharp and harsh than humanly possible.

"Stop saying that," I screamed. "I am not your husband.

"You know nothing of women, Cowan. Saying stop only means do this thing more," Spath softly scolded as he tied the limb to the rope once more.

"Husband, I'm waiting," she called. She stood with her hands on her hips, fingers impatiently tapping.

Even from that distance her face glowered. The Dark Lord himself would have run off into the wilderness to avoid her glare.

"Husband," she called more urgent, angrier, stepping closer to the edge.

"You have my pity, Cowan," Spath whispered.

"Husband," she tormented, stomping her feet.

"Stop saying that," I screamed in return and flung the limb as hard as I could at her. I wanted it to hit her but it dropped harmlessly at her feet.

Bowen picked it up and quickly tied it around her waist.

"If you let go of that rope for a moment, Husband, I will..."

"Yeah, yeah I know, to the ends of the world, hell itself. I got it, I got it."

"Husband Littlefield," she started again. She stood uncertain, peering over the edge.

I yanked the rope. Her scream echoed off the chasm walls followed quickly by a string of threats and curses. Although not a kind act, it gave me a great deal of personal satisfaction. My Jonda friends stood frozen with disbelief. For a few brief moments she hung at the end of the rope, yelling wildly. Slowly, she tired and gave way to silence.

"I think she's dead," Spath whispered. He pulled lightly at the rope with no response.

"I'm holding the rope," I called.

"So help me, pull me up, Mr. Littlefield, now," she growled between clenched teeth.

"Give the rope to me," Spath said, reaching to take my place. "Run, Cowan. This may be your only chance," he said with all earnestness.

"I'm waiting, Mr. Littlefield." Her voice, deep and angry, seemed to claw its way up over the edge and slither along the rope to bite me.

"Pulling, dearest," I said, trembling with an uncertain level of concern. I may have gone too far.

Spath eyes searched mine as he spoke to his two companions. They pulled at the rope, striving to walk backwards to bring her to the top.

I moved to the edge and extended my hand to help her over the top as Spath had me. I hesitated, holding my hand just out of her reach. For that moment, as I looked down into her face, it was as if I was looking into the eternal abyss and it was the Dark Lord's hand that stretched out for me. Her eyes burned with anger as she thrust up her hand for me to grasp.

"Pull me up," she growled.

Her voice sent chills up my spine.

My hand moved of its own volition. My fingers wrapped tightly around her wrist as hers wrapped around mine. I pulled hard and she rose to her waist. I grabbed her arm to pull her the remainder of the way and the ground began to crumble under our weight. Suddenly, we plunged into the gaping fissure. Everyone was yelling at the same time. I clung to Eloise as she kicked wildly. I pulled at her clothing, grappling for the rope about her waist. Just as I forced my hand between her stomach and the rope, we jerked to a stop. My arm felt as though it had been pulled out of its socket. I gasped for air, choking on my heart lodged in my throat.

"Citizen, in my village this is not how we rescue our wives," Spath snickered, peering over the edge. "We men stand up here and pull her to safety."

"Help us, please. I don't know how long I can hold on," I said, hoping the panic in my voice added to the urgency I felt.

"I've got you," Eloise said, holding tightly to me. She swung her body so she could wrap her legs around me, squeezing what little air I had from my lungs. Slowly, agonizingly slowly, they dragged us over the edge to safety. We rolled over one another several times before stopping. Pulling free of the rope, we laughed with relief, hugging each other. Her face glowed with unsurpassed joy and I was overcome with life. I pulled her closer, felt the warmth of her cheek upon mine and then without thought or effort our lips found each other. Hers were inviting, her mouth soft, wonderful. My head swam with desire. I gave the whole of my being to that kiss, as did she. It felt as though a part of my soul was lost to her only to be replaced by a piece of hers. It took my breath away. I tried to focus; to rejoin the world around me as our lips slowly separated. I became aware of the Jonda watching us and of their chuckles at our expense.

"Well, I never," Eloise gasped with embarrassment.

"Well, you kiss like you have," I said, not knowing why. Maybe it was the Jonda laughter or my school boy embarrassment. It seemed right at the time.

Eloise slapped me, hard. She immediately jumped to her feet, brushing the dirt from her clothes. My heart sank and a deep ache took its place. She turned sharply and crossed her arms. Her foot tapped and her jaw flexed as if she where chewing on the angry words that gnawed at her to get out.

"If you aren't too busy, perhaps you could send the rope across," Bowen called from his island prison. The others scampered to retrieve the rope and sent it across.

Bowen tied the rope about Enon and pushed him over the edge. His body swung unimpeded, dead weight, into the embankment on our side. He struck with a dull thud. They pulled at the rope, yanking Enon to safety a few inches at a time.

"Citizen," Spath's voice broke my trance.

"Sorry," I said and sprinted to the edge to help pull Enon to the top.

"I'll do it," Eloise hissed, suddenly by my side. "You know what happened the last time. Wouldn't want you to get carried away and plant one of those sloppy kisses on him. He's suffered enough," she scolded, elbowing at me, pushing her way between the edge and me.

"Even unconscious, he would be a better kisser than you," I said.

"Awh, I never," she cried, releasing her grip on the rope.

"Yeah, you said that."

"Why are you so impossible?" she screeched.

"Just doing the job, that's all,"

"You bastard," she wailed.

"Nag," I countered.

She slapped me again. Her chest heaved, her eyes darted with wild anger.

"Citizen," Spath started.

"Shut up," Eloise and I shouted at the same time.

Spath pointed weakly.

There half above the edge was Enon. Eloise and I ran to pull him up, each of us to a side. We struggled until his body finally slipped over, knocking me down. I sprawled on the ground next to him trying to regain my balance.

"You're not going to kiss him too, are you?" she asked.

"Cayra," Enon whispered.

I looked to Eloise and then Spath.

"Brothers," Bowen's voice came low and hushed. He spoke in Jonda, short, rushed tones.

"What did he say?" I asked.

Spath and the others grabbed Enon, pulling him roughly along the ground. Before I could stand, they had flung the rope and limb across to Bowen. He made no effort to tie himself to the rope but madly threw himself over the side. In a panic, Spath and the others thrust all their effort against the rope, pulling Bowen over the edge like a fish into a boat.

"I said, someone is coming," Bowen spit as he and Spath scooped up Enon and struggled to drag him along. The four of them argued as we rushed headlong toward the basin opening.

We stopped suddenly. They dropped Enon like a bag of unwanted potatoes and argued, straining to hold down their voices. Bowen's voice grew louder than the others. He pounded his chest with his fist several times before thrusting out his hand to them. With its extension the argument was over. Spath was first to take his hand and then the other two placed theirs on top and for a moment not a sound.

"Cayra," each said in turn and the two Jonda trotted off, one in the direction of the dead dog and the other into the darkness.

"Where are they going?" I asked, confused.

"To save us," Bowen said flatly. He and Spath lifted Enon once more and we were off.

I peered into the darkness and listened. Somewhere beyond the basin walls an unidentifiable sound grew louder, someone, a lot of someone's were coming.

Eloise's eyes reflected the genuine fear that gripped my heart. Bowen and Spath struggled to hold Enon up between them, dragging him more than carrying him. His feet stumbled in an effort to support himself as they pulled him along.

There was no sight nor sound of the two Jonda, whether they had escaped or simply hid themselves well, I couldn't tell, but a part of me prayed for their safe return.

The sound was closer now, more distinct, horses, men on horses. The pounding of hooves, their voices and the rattle of weapons echoed off the basin walls. They would breach the opening at any moment.

My heart pounded and Eloise pressed closer to me. A cloud of dust rushed into the basin. From deep inside its heart rode two columns of men with red tunics with silver buttons. They rode the finest horses I had ever seen. They could only be the King's men, all twenty-four of them, riding almost on top of us. We were hemmed in by the massive animals.

From behind the veil of dust, a single horse sped to approach us. It reared as the rider slung his leg over the saddle to dismount before it could come to a stop. It was the King himself.

Enon pulled himself free of Bowen and Spath to meet the advance. He stumbled to the ground, falling on his knees. He struggled to arch his back, pulling up his head and stretched out his arms wide to his side.

The King, propelled by the charge of his horse, rushed to stand in front of Enon. Without hesitation he slammed his fist into Enon's face.

"Where is she?" He screamed and punched him again.

Enon reeled from the blows. Blood dripped from his mouth. The skin under his eye had begun to discolor and swell. He continued to hold out his arms, making no effort to stop the assault or defend himself.

"Where is she?" the King repeated, pulling back his fist for yet another blow.

"He doesn't know," I said, grabbing the King's wrist.

Instantly, the King's men were upon us, swords drawn. At the same moment Spath's dagger appeared at the throat of the King.

"Husband," Eloise gasped, clutching my shoulder.

"Husband?" the King snarled.

"A private joke, nothing more," I said, struggling to maintain my grip on his wrist.

"I could have you all killed with a snap of my fingers," he threatened.

"Not before your blood has the chance to mix with ours," Spath said, pressing his blade a little firmer into the King's neck.

Slowly, Enon rose to his feet, towering above us. "All Jonda hear of today. Sing songs, tell great stories, say Tucker Jonda in here," he said, patting his chest with his fist. "All Jonda children want play Tucker and King. They fight, all want be Tucker. You, when die, just King."

Silence for the moment held us.

Eloise ran her hand over my shoulder as she inched around me. She slid her hand along my arm and to that of the King. Softly, she pulled, separating my grip from his. Then, without warning the King grabbed her arm, a burning anger in his eye.

"Don't ever touch her," I said, yanking his hand free of her.

Everyone flinched with tension once more.

Eloise blushed brightly, her mouth hung open, searching for the words that never came.

"Husband Littlefield has spoken. No one touches his woman," Spath yelled, turning to the King's men. "No one," he intoned softly, turning back to the King.

"Make camp," the King ordered, giving me a look that sent chills down my spine.

"Sire," Eloise started.

"You're one of them now," he said with a sneer and pushed roughly pass her.

"Sire, you are in danger," she pleaded.

He stopped to look at her over his shoulder.

"Chancellor Grimwell," she said, stepping closer to the King.

He turned his head away from her.

She reached out toward him; her hand hovered just beyond his shoulder. It trembled and then a breath before touching him, her fingers withered and hid themselves under her palm.

"Chancellor Grimwell is responsible for Elizabeth's disappearance. He covets your throne and your queen," she said, hanging her head.

"He said you would say that," the King shouted angrily.

"What?" she asked with disbelief.

"My men and I ran into him a short time ago. He told us where we could find you and your treacherous friends."

"He said what? Where is the bastard?" I pressed.

One of the guards stepped between me and the King, pressing his sword against my chest to halt my advance.

"Bastard? He is a hero. He risks his life at this very moment with two of my best men. He rides to return Elizabeth from your evil companion. Your dark plans for my niece end here. He will return by dawn and then you and these Jonda scum will cease to exist. If not by his hand, then surely by mine," the King spat angrily, before stomping off.

"Then, sir, you are a fool and deserve to lose all you have to this monster," I called after him.

Still, he walked away and I began to shake inside with the realization of what had just happened.

"In my village, Brother, no Jonda threatens a King." Spath whispered, slapping a firm hand on my shoulder.

I could only nod my agreement. Without another word, the horses were tethered in a line, dinner fires were started, tents erected, but not for us.

Silently, a post of four men stood sentry about us. We were captives. Enon had slipped into unconsciousness, and lay upon the ground once more.

Eloise stood at the edge of the fire light, her arms folded, her shoulders slumped. It was as if she now carried the weight of the world upon those slender shoulders. She was crying. The King's words had hurt her more than I would have thought possible. It was difficult to think of her as a woman, with all the weakness and frailties that entails. She was as hard and driven as any man I had ever encountered. I had to admire that.

"Here," I said roughly and pushed my kerchief toward her, making sure not to make eye contact. Seeing her cry would most certainly have the same effect on me.

"Thank you," she said softly, allowing her hand to rest on mine for a moment before taking the cloth.   "Sure, any time," I said and started to shuffle my way back to the fire.

"Never seen a woman cry before?" She asked, wiping her face.

"A woman? Sure. You, never."

"You don't see me as a woman?" Her voice was full of hurt and a touch of anger.

"That's not what I meant and you know it," I barked my back still to her.

"You're a hard man, Mr. Littlefield." She sniffed.

"Mr. Littlefield now, is it?" I asked, turning around.

"I only said husband because," she said, rolling the cloth in her hands.

"Because what?"

"I've been... Ruthie was nine when I came to the King's

service. I watched her grow from a shy, clumsy child into a beautiful, graceful woman. Without one of my own, I led my life through hers. Her awkward courtship, her pregnancy, I ached for all of it and then a miracle: Elizabeth. I have been with her every moment of her life. She is my life and my heart is hers. If the King... " She began to cry again.

"He didn't mean it," I said and took her into my arms. "He's just angry. He'll get over it. You'll see."

She sobbed softly into my shoulder as I stroked her hair. I heard no sound, held no thought, and knew only the warmth of her body against mine. Time stood still for us. There was no King, no Norha, and no Kathryn. Even the Jonda were pushed from my mind.

At that moment she was the entirety of my universe. Standing there in the darkness, holding her, filled me with feelings I had thought long dead. I was drowning in desire. There has never been time for a woman, no room in my meager existence for a wife, for children, for family. I suddenly felt cheated by life, empty, save for the warmth of her in my arms. It poured into me, filling me.

"You're pulling my hair," she groused.

"I'm sorry, what?" I asked, trying to swim back to the real world.

"Ow. My hair, you clod, you're pulling it," she shrieked.

The buttons on my cuff had somehow managed to tangle themselves.

"Ow! Stop it. Don't pull it. You're making it worse. Ow! Ow!" she cried.

"Hold still, you old cow, let me do it," I said, grappling with my coat to remove it.

The more effort I gave, the more she yelled. Finally, she pulled in one direction and I in the other.

"OOOOW! You bastard, you did that on purpose," she screamed and then pummeled me repeatedly with her fist.

I stumbled backwards, trying to avoid her attack, falling to the ground. Her yowl had been accompanied by the unmistakable sound of hair ripping from her skull. A large tangle of it hung from my cuff.

"Are you insane? What is wrong with you?" I asked, scrambling to my feet.

"You, you're what's wrong with me. The moment I let my

guard down you're pawing me or trying to scalp me."

"I wasn't trying to scalp you, you old bat."

"Old... " she gasped. Her face turned red. Her lips gyrated wildly from side to side as if her tongue were sorting out the words she was about to spit. "Old is it? At least I'm not an ugly, middle aged, balding, worthless lay about."

"Well, you are now," I said and held up the wad of hair hanging from my cuff.

"Well, I never, you bastard," she screamed in my face and slapped me. It seemed harder this time than the last. I kind of liked it.

"You said that before," I called after her. "I didn't believe it then and I don't believe it now."

"Monster," she screamed, bending to pick up a rock and throwing it at me.

"Takes one to know one," I said and threw a rock back at her.

"Demon, bastard, devil," she stammered and threw another rock.

"I couldn't be the devil. He's your true husband. It wasn't called Hell until you got there. He doubtless sent you back just to get some peace and quiet, anything to escape your nagging."

"I... I... OH!" she cried in frustration and threw one last rock before stomping off toward the fire. She grumbled passionately to herself, kicking at the dirt along the way. Her every movement was exaggerated by the depth of her anger. The Jonda, not a foolhardy people, stepped politely out of her way.

I stood for a moment looking up at the stars, blinking in soft colors. They washed across the night sky like spilled salt across a black tablecloth. I tried to shut out the sounds of the acid, the horses, the King's men and Eloise. I stood there waiting, she couldn't be angry forever.

After a while, she calmed down and the King's men brought us blankets and food, or at least something close to it. We sat quietly and ate, each ignoring the other. The bread was so hard that stale would have been an improvement. The soup, a generous and erroneous label, was more water than cuisine. Strange, colored bits of something floated languidly just under its surface. Its smell, its flavor was best not discussed in mixed company.

"This is terrible," said Eloise, setting her bowl to the ground.

"I've had worse," I lied.

"Nothing could be worse than this," she countered.

"I don't know. Do you cook?" I asked. I tried to put a little lilt in my voice so she would know I was joking.

Without lifting their eyes from their bowls, Bowen and Spath slid back on their barrels away from her at the same time.

"I was joking," I said, trying to recover.

"No. You weren't," she said, her voice full of hurt.

"I was," I said, staring into my bowl. I tried to gag down one last bite of bread. I softened it in the glop now coagulating in the bottom of my bowl.

"No. You were being mean-spirited at my expense," she said sourly.

"Sorry," I said as apologetically as I could.

"Not enough for me," she quipped.

"Fine, have it your way," I said, standing, tossing away my bowl. I'd had enough. I snapped the blanket and kicked away a handful of rocks, smoothing the soil with my foot as best I could for a place to lie down. I lay facing the fire, feeling its comforting warmth. If I could just get some sleep, I could shut it all out.

"I was going to lie there," Eloise said, punctuating her words with a heavy kick to my back.

"My good woman, are you insane? Go lie down anywhere you want, just leave me alone," I groused.

"I want to lie there," she protested.

"Well, you can't. Now leave me alone," I said harshly and pulled the loose ends of the blanket over myself.

She promptly threw her blanket between me and the fire and lay down.

"What are you doing?"

"I'm doing what you said. I'm laying down anywhere I want."

"You're blocking the fire."

"Am I? I hadn't noticed."

"You're doing it deliberately."

"And what if I am?"

"Our Cowan is afraid of the dark," Spath snickered.

"I am not. I didn't want it to go out, that's all," I barked, perhaps a little too defensively.

That was the end of it, nothing else was said. I rolled over in a huff and tried to go to sleep.

I began to drift, soft images blurring my mind, carrying me off to dream land. I was jarred back to reality for a moment. Eloise had rolled against me. She pulled herself up to lie in my arms, her head cradled in my shoulder, her hand resting warmly in the center of my chest. I smiled softly to myself before drowning in the smell of her hair and sank gladly into the bottomless darkness of sleep.

Chapter 9

"Tucker."

The word filtered into my mind. My body ached; my joints were stiff and my head pounded. Something pressed heavily against my chest. Without opening my eyes, the images of Eloise lying in my arms from the night before filled my mind.

I murmured the endearments that swam between my heart and my thought. I whispered from the depth of my soul, of the ache from all the empty years.

"I like you also, Brother," Bowen's voice pulled at me.

I struggled to focus, to wake up.

"What?" I asked confused.

He pulled me, helping me to sit up.

"I like you also," he repeated.

The fire had died too little more than embers. Eloise laid with her back to me, huddled under her blanket, the curve of her hip pulling it tight. Her head was propped up on a piece of firewood. She snored loudly.

"What's happening?" I asked, pulling at the blanket. Only then did I notice that neither Enon nor Spath was anywhere to be seen.

"We must go," Bowen whispered, inching closer.

"Go where?" I asked, matching his tone.

He smiled broadly, turning slightly to his left, and pointed to the top of the basin. I rubbed my eyes, trying to focus. From the edge of those shadows, a rope slowly snaked its way down the steep wall to the bottom.

"Now, Brother, is it you, brother of the Jonda, or the joy of your life we send first?" he teased.

"It's bad enough to have Spath torment me. Must you?" I groused and lay back down.

"Norha stomachs are seldom full, Brother, and you have pricked their hunger," he said, feeling the meat of my leg.

"Stop that," I said angrily, slapping at his hand.

"Can you hear that?" he asked, sinking lower.

I strained, listening. That sound, it was familiar. Somewhere in the distance the Roar of the Bear cut through the darkness. They were returning. There had to be hundreds of them, all making that horrible noise.

Close to the basin opening, the King barked orders to his men.

"Let no Jonda enter this bastion. Take no prisoners," he called.

My heart sank with his words.

"Our brothers have returned. Enon is safe, Spath is safe. Now we must go. The King has guests for breakfast," Bowen said, pulling me to my feet.

"Be you Jonda or friend? Ride forth and show yourself," the King ordered, standing in the mouth of the opening, his sword in one hand and a torch in the other. Behind him, his men lined up as if all were geese and he the one that knew where south lay.

"He thinks they're Jonda?"

"He does, Brother. We must go," Bowen said urgently, heaving at me.

"We can't leave him," Eloise said, pulling herself upright.

"Take her first," I said. I took her hand and helped her to her feet.

"I won't go without the King," she said as she pulled her hand from mine.

I began to ask her if she had gone mad but was stopped before I could utter a single word.

"We can't leave him behind, not knowing what we know about them."

"What do you want me to do?" I asked, lost.

"I don't know," she mouthed weakly. "Something," she said, laying her hand on my arm lightly.

We both looked to Bowen for an answer. His face held a blank expression. Slowly we followed his eyes to the rope.

"Take her," I said, pushing her toward Bowen.

"Husband," she called softly.

I pretended not to hear. I walked swiftly in the direction of the King.

"I must be out of my mind," I said to myself.

Ahead of me, one of the King's men turned to meet my advance. "Sire," he called over his shoulder, planting his feet wide and drawing his sword.

The King turned to look at me and then turned away without a word.

"Sire, you and your men are in terrible danger. They are the Norha, not Jonda,"

"I would expect you to say that. They will rescue you soon enough," he spit angrily.

"You are wrong, Sire. If they were Jonda why would they still be up there?" I asked, turning to point to the top of the basin.

The King peered into the darkness. His eyes searched for the evidence of which I spoke. He gave me an icy glare before turning to the opening in the wall once more.

"Sire," a voice drifted through to us.

"Grimwell," the King said with relief.

His men breathed a level of encouragement to one another.

"Sire," I said as the muscles in my stomach tightened into a horrible knot. "If it is Grimwell and your men, he if anyone would ride in unimpeded, would he not?"

Everyone's attention turned to the King, waiting for his response.

I had passed the knot from my stomach to theirs.

"Perhaps the Jonda hold him captive," a man said, half to himself, half to his comrades.

The King's face twisted with the thoughts that must have been coursing through his mind. His eyes searched the faces of all present and then spun toward the opening again.

"Grimwell, are you safe? Do the Jonda hold you against your will?" he asked his voice weaker, more hesitant than before.

From beyond the opening a single voice answered.

"There are no Jonda here, Sire," Grimwell smirked from the darkness.

The tone in his voice held a level of malice that shook me to the core.

"Sire," I said, walking to his side.

He held his torch over his head, peering deep into the dark mouth as if trying to divine the future.

I stared over his shoulder, at the opposite end... first just a few and then more and then more still... the faint glimmer, the reflection, and the yellow eyes of the Norha.

"My men," he said, swinging around to me, full of belief.

The knot in my stomach jumped to my throat and I ran.

"To your horses," he suddenly screamed, and everyone ran.

Several of the men reached their horses and galloped to the opening, riding in a tight cluster, in hopes of forcing their way to freedom. Their illusion of escape crumpled at the far end as the Norha fell upon them. The sounds of their fighting echoed off the walls eerily. They were fighting for their lives. The horse's cries of anguish mixed with those of the King's men. The ghoulish delight the Norha voices took in their mayhem chilled me to the bone. More of the men rode in, either to escape or to join in the battle. I didn't know which. I didn't look back. I didn't want to see.

The King and three of his men were last to reach their horses. His horse reared and spun as he mounted before they thundered past me.

The King sprang to the front of the charge, his sword slicing the air wildly.

Beyond the basin walls Grimwell roared, driving the Norha into the opening from his side. On our side, the opening was becoming clogged with the bodies of the Norha, the horses and the King's men.

The Norha had breached the opening and poured into our side like water through a dam, squeezing past the bodies of the dead and dying. They were suddenly everywhere.

The King and the three that rode with him slew them as fast as their swords could swing. More entered to take their place and still more crushed forward to follow them. There were too many to count. They pulled at the King and his men, trying to dismount them, grabbing the legs of man and horse alike.

The King's horse screamed and rose repeatedly to stomp many of them to death before breaking free. Driven by fear – or by the King - I could not say, but it ran. The Norha fell to its passing and the horses of the three guards followed its lead.

The Norha howled their anger and gave chase.

"Reach for me," the King screamed as he charged toward me. He leaned half out of his saddle, his right arm outstretched and his eyes full of the madness around us. I grabbed frantically for his arm, terrified that I would miss and be left to the Norha or be trampled under the horse itself. Drawn by the power of the horse's passing, I was flung upon its back behind the King almost at the instant I touched his arm. It charged with an amazing strength. Its body rippled with muscle under us. It knew the mind of its master.

Beyond my belief, he drove the animal toward the chasm. My mind raced; do I jump or do I... ? There was no time.

The horse launched us into the air, jumping the abyss we had escaped but hours before.

We landed hard on the opposite side. The horse stumbled and I was thrown to the ground, as was the King. As I rolled to a stop, the three that followed our lead were in midair. I covered my face with my arms and prayed they wouldn't land on me. The first thundered to my right and I pushed hard to get to my feet. The second landed only a moment after as I scurried to evade its assault. Time seemed to slow as the third, its front half falling on solid ground and its back flailing wildly at the soft edge. Before we could speak the edge began to give way. The horse screamed its eyes wide beyond imagination and full of fear, as it fought to gain its balance. The realization of his fate spread quickly across the man's face. His mouth opened wide but uttered no sound. I blinked in disbelief as horse and rider fell backward into the trench, crashing to the bottom.

The Norha rushed to the edge and roared with delight at the poor man's misfortune. They began to throw sticks and rocks at us, angry at our escape.

"Poor devil," the King said, turning to me.

The jeers of the Norha increased in volume and pace. The sound of the Roar of the White Bear hammered fear into the very core of me. Slowly, they cleared a path and Grimwell himself made his way through the throng.

"Sire," he snarled.

"Why, Grimwell? I treated you like family," the King demanded across the divide.

"Family? I was your pet, listening to your petty concerns. You were never a king. You were a buffoon. Now, I will be king, a king to be reckoned with," he hissed.

"I will die before I will allow you to take my throne," the King promised.

"I will see to it myself," Grimwell said, waving his hand in dismissal. "Imagine how the Queen will feel when I bring the sad news of your death and that of your niece. I'm sure she will fall, washed away in grief, into my arms for comfort."

"You will never live long enough to enjoy it. I will raise from the grave, walk the world as a ghost. I will find you and I will give my soul to any who will have it but I will reach into your throat and pull your beating heart out with my own hand," the King cursed.

"Please have the good manners to wait until we've finished having sex," Grimwell chided.

At that moment two ropes, thrown from above, bounced to a stop just behind us. Grimwell saw them at the same moment I did.

"Stop them, you fools! Don't let them escape. Stop them now," he bellowed.

The Norha instantly reacted. Many of them screamed and threw stones. The majority ran to the opening, retrieving the bodies of the dead – man, horse and Norha alike – only to return and pitch them, one after another into the bottom of the trench.

"Come then, you bastards, come. I have steel enough for all of you," the King roared angrily, waving his sword. With his free hand, he deflected many of the stones thrown and shook his fist.

"The top, you idiots, find them, kill them. Kill them all," Grimwell roared.

Half of the Norha ran to the opening to cut off our salvation.

The two guards looked briefly to one another as if exchanging the same thought between them. Each nodded to other and then the older of the two did the unthinkable. He grabbed the King by his shoulder and spun him about to face him.

With staggering strength, the elder man flung his whole weight into a punch... square into the King's face.

The King reeled, staggering backward a few steps. His eyes burned with madness and I saw the death of the man play out across his face.

"Forgive me, Sire," he stammered before the King could

react. "I had meant to render you unconscious. I had no idea you could take such a... " His voice trailed off. His eyes darted between the ground and the King.

"Why?" The King asked, wiping the blood from his mouth.

"I only wished to save you from yourself, Sire," he said apologetically.

The King rubbed his chin, coming closer to the younger man, rolling his sword repeatedly in his hand.

"Go on," the King mumbled, flexing his jaw repeatedly.

"I, we," he said, nodding to the other man, "vowed to protect you with our lives. If you stay, you will die and that monster will have the lives of the entire kingdom within his palm, including those of our families, both yours and mine. I thought if I could render you unconscious, Mr. Littlefield could take you to safety."

"I can't run away," the King said softly, placing his hand on the younger man's shoulder.

"No one thinks you a coward, Sire. If you live you may yet stop this insanity."

The King's face softened greatly. He glanced briefly in my direction and then over his shoulder to the Norha and to Grimwell. They were gaining. They would reach us soon.

Grimwell paced briskly, his eyes never leaving the King.

I grabbed the ropes, tying the first about my waist and held the second.

"I will make your son the captain of my guard," the King said with deep sadness, pulling his hand from his shoulder with a soft pat.

"If my son is to be captain of the guard, he will earn it himself. I ask only that he and his mother not go hungry and that you hold them in fair opinion," the elder man said, pulling back, his shoulders straight.

"You have my word, as you're King, as your friend, and with my respect."

"Sire," I said, holding out the rope to him.

He moved closer, stopping short of grabbing the rope. He stood, stiff, unmoving, facing me, his back to the younger men, theirs to his. He bounced the sword in his hand again and again.

"Sire," I repeated, extending the rope once more.

"I cannot go," he said.

"Hurry, Sire. We will hold them for as long as we can," the young man said. His voice quivered slightly.

I didn't know what to do, what to say. The Norha were gaining. They would cross the divide in moments. I looked up the length of rope that led to safety, its origin lost in the darkness. Did they see me? Did they know?

"Run, coward, run," Grimwell called from across the trench. "I will find you and end your miserable, small existence, no matter in what hole you hide."

The King's face reddened, his jaw twitched, the muscle flexing hard under his skin. He bounced the sword faster now. His entire body shook with the anger he tried to hold inside.

I moved to stand in front of him.

"My pardon, Sire," I whispered and slipped the rope about his waist. "He's an ass. Don't listen to him," I said and tied the rope tightly about him. My mind raced. Several of the Norha, their fingers greedily clawing at the edge of the dirt on our side, would pull themselves to the top in moments.

"Don't you understand? I can't go," he whispered.

"Well, ordinarily I would agree, given a third choice. For me, if I escape before one of those bastards can get me, then waiting at the top of this rope is the Governess. Who, as you know, can be... "

"Difficult," the King said with a smile.

"Not the word I had in mind but you understand my situation. If I escaped without you, well, I can only imagine. If I am not eaten alive by one, then I surely will be by the other."

Those at the top unexpectedly pulled the rope tied to me and I was yanked off the ground, rising several feet above the King and then he, now tethered to the rope, abruptly followed.

As we spun slowly in the air, four of the Norha pulled their way to the top. Those on the other side cheered wildly at their success.

The four, beating their chest in front of the two guards, edged closer before suddenly charging. The King's men cut them down quickly and they were no more. The Norha roared their anger and more of them poured into the abyss.

They climbed over the dead, over one another, standing on shoulders, pitching each higher than the last until they reached the edge and the blades of the King's last defense.

Driven on by the Chancellor, more of the Norha scrambled to reach us. They poured into the gorge like the soft sand. A Norha fell with each swing of the guard's swords. When one fell, two more took their place and another four when those fell to their steel.

From above, the faint sound of fighting drifted down to us. Something warm rained down, it was thick, sticky and smelled terrible. It took me a moment to realize that it was blood. At the instant of clarity, the body of a Norha rushed past us from above, smashing to the ground with a sickening thud. I looked up just in time to see another body freefalling toward me. It struck me in its passing to join the first; forcing me to swing back and forth wildly as several more flew by to join the first two.

Again the rope was yanked and I jerked several feet ahead of the King and he followed. He dangled just below me. Again and again the rope pulled at my midsection.

Below, the Norha had crawled over the edge like an army of ants, all intent on one goal. They pressed their numbers to overwhelming odds, yet the guards fought on with unthinkable prowess. The ropes jerked and we lurched upward once more, leaving them to fend for themselves. Several of the Norha tried and failed to climb the steep walls. Others threw themselves at the King and at me, slamming themselves into the stone face in an effort to reach us. At last, thrown into the air by his fellows, one of the Norha attached himself to the King's leg. They spun wildly as they fought. The Norha attempted to claw his way up the King's body. The King beat him with the hilt of his sword, trying to break free, but the Norha clung with uncanny determination. To my horror, the King's attacker maneuvered himself to crawl up his back. The creature slipped his arm around the King's neck, trying desperately to snap it. In an attempt to free himself the King hammered his elbow repeatedly into the ribs of the Norha.

They struggled with one another, swinging in ever-wider arcs. I kicked off the wall and grabbed the length of hair at the back of the Norha's head. I yanked it with all my strength.

He refused to let go. He roared at me, revealing jagged, uneven teeth. He swiped at me with his free hand, clinging stubbornly to the King's back. I pulled once more, spinning us, tangling our ropes briefly and then spun back, freeing them again. The Norha's grip loosened from the King's neck, slipping to his collar. He pulled himself up, screaming, pressing his feet into the King's back.

He leapt, bridging the distance in less than a heart beat, grabbing hold of me, digging his fingers into my chest and back, climbing me as he did the King. The rope that tried to pull me in half, now threatened to succeed with the added weight of the madman clutching my flesh through my clothing. His hands, his arms were more powerful than any natural creature. My heart pitched into my throat and pounded so hard I feared it would fall out of my mouth. The monster clung to me, grasping unfathomable handfuls of my flesh. He reached up to grab the rope, steadying himself, wrapping his muscular legs around me. He drew a clenched fist back, twisting his body in an unnatural way. His arm, heavily cabled, muscled, rippled like a snake as the energy of his hate focused on me. I wanted to close my eyes but could not. I could only hold my breath.

At that moment, another body thrown from above slammed into us knocking the Norha free of me. As he fell, the creature turned, spinning back toward the King. He grasped wildly at the King's clothing, clawing his way down, gaining and losing his hand hold almost simultaneously. He made one last desperate attempt to save himself, and succeeded. Time stood still as he, with one hand, dangled from the King's right foot. His head turned to look down and then slowly turned up to the King.

A wicked, sick smile crossed his thin lips and he flung his free hand up to grasp the King's leg, pulling himself up, climbing as if it were a rope.

The King kicked wildly at the monster but to no avail. It climbed steadily upward, its smile growing broader with each new hand grip, each new success.

I pushed hard off the wall, forcing my body to swing into them. I made every effort to set my feet into the creature's back, kicking it as hard as I could.

It roared in pain, arching back but clung to the King all

the more. Its head spun to glare at me, its eyes burned with anger, its teeth mashed with hate.

It began to climb again, now with more determination.

Again, I pushed off the wall, positioning myself to dislodge the Norha with my feet.

Again, I kicked the creature, bringing all the force I had to bear into its spine.

It roared, releasing his hold with one hand, spinning back toward me, reaching out to grasp the air where my leg had been but moments before. It returned its hold, striving for the King's neck once more, climbing faster than before. I was the pendulum; my swing to safety short lived. This time, upon my return, the Norha seized my leg before I could strike. It yanked hard; all but pulling my leg from its socket as it transferred its weight to me. We swung away from the King briefly as it started its ascent up my body. I fought back with all I had, smashing my fist into his face with all my strength, but to little or no avail.

In return, it punched and bit me, tearing bits of clothing and flesh with each new mouthful. It was merciless in its attack. It meant to kill me.

I screamed in horrible pain as blood flowed from each new wound it savaged upon me. Blood soaked my clothing. It was everywhere. I closed my eyes, screaming, and wracked in agony.

When I opened them again the monstrosity was nose to nose with me. It roared its hate, its anger, into my face as I screamed in torment.

Then suddenly, its face shifted, twisting with new anguish. Its grip loosened. It tried to look back over its shoulder to the King. Following its gaze, I stared into the King's grim face. As we swung back to the King, he had thrust his sword into the creature's back. It attempted to howl its torment but could only gurgle as blood oozed from its mouth.

It turned back to me, moving its face closer to my own, its eyes narrowed. Blood spilled from its mouth down my chest and then slowly the monster fell away. Free of its weight, I drew a deep breath, clenching my teeth to subdue the pain.

The rope jerked again and we inched closer to the top. At last, we were pulled to safety, to the top of the basin. I glanced to the bottom in hopes of seeing the two young guards still standing their ground. Instead, the Norha swarmed over the spot where they last stood, writhing like maggots covering a rotting piece of meat.

Eloise threw her arms around me and sobbed. She washed my face with her tears, covering every inch with her kisses. The damage I endured faded to the back of my mind. I held her in my arms and melted into her warmth.

Much too soon, she pulled away and held out her arms to the King, hesitating briefly, not knowing if she should or not. He hung his head and limply held out his arms in return. They hugged and cried.

I shifted my eyes away from them for fear that I too would break down uncontrollably. Blood soaked the ground. Piles of dead Norha surrounded us, more than I could count. My stomach pitched.

At the center of this nightmare, thirty or so Jonda stood, shoulder to shoulder, their chests heaving. Giant men, faces and bodies covered in blood and paint, waiting for the next wave of Norha. Each held a large stick with three prongs, a round stone the size of a large fist, tied to its center. Norha blood painted the length of each crude weapon and the better part of each man's arms.

Among the trees, ten, perhaps fifteen, Norha edged closer, waiting for an opportunity or more of their kind. The Jonda shifted restlessly, scouring the woods for more of the vile creatures.

The King pulled free of Eloise, breaking her hold, wiping his face, as did she.

"Kaowa ky," came a voice that sounded like Bowen's.

I peered through the trees of men, searching for a glimpse of him. After a moment we made eye-contact.

"We ride," he called again, this time speaking in common.

We were suddenly surrounded by the Jonda, brushed about by their abrupt activity. One of them grabbed me as if I were a child and threw me atop one of the horses, a massive animal fit for giant men. Huge painted hand prints decorated their flanks, the color matching its rider.

Eloise was treated the same and placed behind me. The King, either on his own or helped as were we, sat alone atop a black steed. He looked as if he belonged.

For a brief moment, the two of us exchanged a look, his face a mirror of the sorrow that swept through me. The beast he rode, happy for the weight of a rider, rose up, and eager to run. From this perch, he turned a tight circle, making one last search of the bodies for the good Chancellor.

"We ride," Bowen's voice called again and the horses burst into the dappled morning light.

Eloise wrapped her arms around me, clutching me tight. It felt good.

We rode, surrounded by the Jonda, thundering through the woods. The few Norha that tried to stop us were dealt with swiftly and harshly. None could stand before the Jonda's assault, but they followed, running with amazing strength and speed, almost as fast as our horses.

From seemingly nowhere, more Jonda joined our escape, cutting down those Norha that followed our passing. We numbered more than fifty now and, as we rode, our numbers grew. They came from nowhere, from everywhere.

The King, Eloise and I rode at the center of a growing hoard, safe within the eye of this storm of giant horses, ridden by giant men. She laid her cheek against my back, her tears soaking my clothing, her soft sobs pulling at me. I clenched my teeth, trying to hold back my own pain and my tears. The patches of missing flesh, my clothing, now turned black, was encrusted with dried blood.

I didn't care, as long as her arms were around me and the black sand, the Norha, the insanity, was all behind us... far, far behind us.

Chapter 10

We rode in silence; only the thundering of hooves spoke to us. Hours passed in this manner. Eventually, the trees dropped away and the ground lay out flat to become softly rolling hills, covered in tall grass. The grass waved gently in the morning air, as if the swells of the ocean moved beneath. Small yellow and blue flowers littered all for as far as the eye could see.

Beyond this heaven, over the last hill, a group of five trees stood alone, offering us shade and a chance to rest. Under these trees no grass grew, only a dark soil and a scattering of leaves.

We followed Bowen and dismounted in the shade. Eloise slipped off first to help me down. My body ached and my joints were stiff, almost beyond use.

The Jonda rode a full circle around the trees before dividing into groups and makeshift camps. The horses, now covered in foam, grazed between ragged breaths, stomping listlessly.

Eloise smoothed her hand over my back as we sought a place to rest under the nearest tree. As we were about to sit down, a straggler, a lone Jonda rider made his way to Bowen.

"I didn't get the chance to say thank you," the King said, holding out his hand to me, suddenly there.

I took his hand and shook it softly, not knowing what to say.

"You should be proud, Eloise," he said sadly.

She nodded in response, wiping a tear from her face, her arm wrapped tightly about me.

"I would like you to have this," he said, holding out his sword to me. "It was my father's, father's, passed down to me upon my conformation."

The hilt of twisted gold, encrusted in jewels, sparkled bright under the thick Norha blood. The blade, double-edged steel, had channeled the thick fluid down its edge. It glinted in the morning light and even when covered in dried blood it was a beautiful thing.

"Very generous, Sire, but I could not. I'm no soldier, no fighter. It would only mean hardship and one battle after another until I lost it or it was taken from me," I said honestly.

"Then perhaps this," he offered, holding out his dagger. Although only eight inches or so in length and plain by comparison, it was the most beautiful object I had ever seen. My hand trembled slightly as it passed from his to mine. It fell to the ground. As I stooped to retrieve it, he did the same.

The letter Eloise had given me on that first night so long ago fell to the ground as well. I reached for the paper. Eloise's hand was suddenly, gently there. She smoothed her hand over mine, closing hers tightly, half over the paper, holding mine closed as well.

The King lifted the dagger, eyeing the paper with curiosity.

"And what is this?" he asked, straightening.

"Nothing, Sire," Eloise said quickly.

He looked to me as if for the truth and I looked to her. Her eyes looked deep inside me, pleading. Her face, wet with tears and the blood that covered me, looked suddenly worried.

"Nothing, Sire," I echoed, my eyes locked on hers.

Eloise smiled, squeezing my hand tightly, rubbing my back with affection.

"Be proud, Eloise," he repeated, handing her the dagger.

"I am, Sire," she said, taking it from him.

I slipped the paper back into my pocket.

Eloise handed me the dagger and I slid it into the seam at the side of my boot with a grateful smile. It was a perfect fit.

The King turned away, satisfied.

Eloise rested her hand on my chest, patting the letters in my pocket softly.

"Thank you," she said, laying her head on my shoulder, starting to cry again, more softly this time.

I could never understand women and this one was both ends of the rainbow at the same time. I held her close and we rocked slowly in each other's arms. My head swam with the thought of her, with all that had happened and all things that burned within me. Thousands of words suddenly poured into my head as I tried to sort them out.

"They're looking at us," Eloise whispered.

"I don't care," I replied and kissed her. We stood and rocked. I had no concept of time or of my place in the world, just her arms around me.

"They're still looking," she said, turning me toward the Jonda. I stared over her shoulder. Bowen and four others hunkered close to the ground. Standing over them was the lone rider and the rest of the Jonda. No one spoke, not even to each other. All appeared to be looking in our direction.

"Brother," Bowen said, standing, coming our way.

I pulled reluctantly away from Eloise.

"Brother," he repeated. "These men will scout our safe passage," he said, signaling the others. The four men that had crouched to the ground with him presented themselves. Each was lean, muscular and wore faces of stern determination. They stood several feet away. Their posture seemed odd, rigid almost or ill at ease. Something felt wrong. Eloise sensed it too; she shifted to stand behind me, still holding my hand.

"Good," I said and waited for the other shoe to drop. The stiffness of the dagger in my boot jumped to the forefront of my mind.

"Brother," Bowen said with hesitation, looking at the ground. "We are still in danger's way. They will ride to the four winds, searching for the Norha, whose nation now searches for us."

I didn't know where he was going with this or what it had to do with me. He refused to make eye contact.

"You think they're still following us?" I asked.

"Our spy says yes. They will stand in this very spot before the sun falls this night. He says they have sent runners to She Who Hunts. The Chancellor has... all Norha are to find you... and bring your head to him," he said without looking up.

Eloise gasped quietly, lowering her head to my shoulder, and squeezed my hand.

"How can you be sure?"

"I am sure, Brother."

"It just keeps getting better and better," I said, turning to Eloise. My mind reeled with confusion. I pulled my hand away from her, roughly. "You couldn't just let me be, could you?"

"You're blaming me?" she asked with disdain.

"Yes, I am. My life wasn't like this until I met you. I didn't have Norha chasing me up ropes to chew on me, people stabbing me, branding me, and pursuing me all over hell and back. I knew better than to get involved with you. I told myself, 'stay away from this one, Tucker' but did I listen? Oh no, not me," I ranted.

"You are... You are blaming me," she said, irritated. Her eyes grew large, her face red.

"Brother, perhaps at another time. These men... " Bowen said, pulling at my shoulder.

Eloise and I stood nose to nose and glared.

"He's talking to you but you wouldn't know that because it's my entire fault."

"Governess," the King's voice boomed angrily, startling us both.

Her eyes instantly met his and burned with anger. Her jaw flexed without uttering a word, his stern expression holding her in check.

"Brother, there is little time. The men must go," Bowen said earnestly.

"What are they waiting for?" I asked, annoyed.

Bowen glanced to the men briefly and then to me.

"Your good will, Brother," he said, stepping closer.

"My good will?" I asked, more confused now than before. I looked about as if the answer lay in the face of one or of all present.

"Everyone here saw what you did," he said, sweeping his hand across the circle of Jonda that surrounded us. "You are the Soul Bearer and you took no Norha. Not one. Not even the one that tried to kill you, tried to kill the King. Such things cannot go unnoticed."

I shifted uncomfortably.

"To the heart of it, Brother, they seek your protection," he said abruptly, tightly pulling back his shoulders as if he asked for the moon.

"They have whatever I can do," I said wholeheartedly.

A murmur of voices spread quickly through the Jonda and the four riders stepped closer.

"Brother, I..." Bowen said, his voice quivering slightly. He gripped my arm firmly and threw his free arm about me, hugging me tightly.

His eyes darted back and forth as if searching my face for some sign, some glint of understanding. "Make no sound, show no pain," he whispered, gripping my arm more firmly. He pulled me closer and then jabbed his fingers into my wound. The blood flowed freely once more.

"What the hell's wrong with you?" I asked between clenched teeth, trying to break free of his grip.

He held his fingers, wet with my blood, high over his head.

The Jonda cheered.

The four riders, each in turn, stepped forward to do the same. Each pressed their fingers deep into my wound and then held their bloody trophy high for all to see. The surrounding Jonda cheered madly as the riders, one after the other, wiped the blood from their fingers, marking their faces with it. The cheering grew louder as the four men mounted their horses and rode away, each in one of the four directions.

The Jonda stood with their backs to me as the riders vanished over the far horizon. Blood oozed from between my fingers as I held my hand over the newly opened wound, trying to understand these strange people, their strange customs. Bowen turned to face me. He stared deep into my eyes, his face serious, and his eyes stern. Slowly, without a word his hand came to his face, wiping my blood in long streaks from under his eyes to his jaw.

"Kaowa ky," he called and the men were a blur of activity again.

With no small help I mounted the animal again. This time Eloise rode with the King. My heart filled with a deep ache as she wrapped her arms about him and then rode away.

We traveled for what seemed like forever, well past midday. Bowen at the head of this throng stood in his saddle and turned to those behind. He whistled and waved his hand and half the riders split off and galloped west without breaking stride. I squinted into the afternoon sun after them. Did they ride to their safety or to ours? I looked to Eloise and the King for some reaction. She glanced in my direction only briefly, and then turned away.

My body, jarred with each new rise and fall of the horse, felt every bruise, every strain placed upon it. I hoped the animal would tire soon. I struggled to balance in my saddle as sleep pulled at me even here. The sun slipped below the horizon and twilight covered the land. We had to stop soon. Again, Bowen whistled and again, half of the men turned west and rode off into the growing dark. We didn't stop after they disappeared.

Behind us, on the very edge of sight, the faint light of torches – Norha torches – were still there, still following. I looked over my shoulder at every chance, watching the dull glow come closer.

Hours passed and then the torches split, half following our fellows and the remainder following us.

As the night grew older and the moon rose high over the landscape, again Bowen signaled and more Jonda rode west. We were but a thin shadow of our beginning. No one spoke. No one looked left or right, only ahead, only north, only into the darkness.

I poured all of my effort, all my will into staying awake, to staying in the saddle, fatigue, weariness, sleep fought for dominion over my body and mind.

My horse breathed laboriously, and at long last we slowed. We did not stop but merely trotted. I bounced in the saddle deliberately in an effort to stay awake. After a short while, much too short a while, we began again and again we halved. We continued north and they to the west. With expectation, knowing the future before it came to pass, I watched over my shoulder, through the haze now clogging my mind, as the single path of torches became two, one west and the other unrelentingly following us north. We were little more than five Jonda, Bowen, the King, Eloise and I.

I closed my eyes, swaying with the movement of the horse, praying for the chance to sleep and the hours continued to slip away. As I was about to fall off from exhaustion, through the muddled fog that filled by head, a horse and rider drew close to me.

"A gift for you, Brother," the voice said with excitement.

My mind swam with confusion. Next to me rode one of the four riders, now returned. He rode close, holding out his arm to me.

Something hung from his fist, swinging in the night air. I reached out, out of reflex, and took it from his hand.

"With my thanks," he yelled and rode ahead to join Bowen.

I tried to focus in the dark on the object. It swung loosely in my grip, tied with a small leather band. In the moonlight, my gift revealed itself. To my shock, my horror, it was hair... Norha hair and at one end, holding the thick clump together as a single mass was skin. My mind flooded with a mixture of emotions. I glanced down to the hole the Norha had bitten into my leg, smiled weakly to myself and stuffed the offering, skin and all, under the front of my saddle.

With the addition of our scout, Bowen turned in his saddle, and called out softly. At long last the horses slowed to a walk and I gave a grateful sigh, as did the others.

The Jonda spoke quietly between themselves. Off and on, each of them turned to look at me, smiling, gesturing to each other, their voices light, animated.

They nodded to me as if they were passing to say good morning.

From behind, more riders trotted up to join us, all very happy, almost nonchalant in manner, most covered in fresh blood. All sense of urgency was now gone.

I looked behind for any sign of the Norha.

The faint glow of their torches that had shown on the horizon had now disappeared altogether. Shortly, more Jonda riders returned. Our numbers were growing again.

At the head of this group, another scout also returned with a Norha gift... the same Norha gift. I added it to the first with a nod and a tired smile.

With the setting of the moon, the balance of the Jonda had returned and with the appearance of each rider of the four winds, a new clump of Norha hair embellished my saddle.

"Nev'ah Kaowa ky," Bowen said his voice loud, strong, and buoyant. The Jonda spoke to one another, laughing. Our horses walked slowly, almost meandering. All who had rode west had circled back to rid us of the Norha and then joined the previous group to hunt them down, eliminating one small group at a time, before returning to us. By all accounts, we were whole again.

Eloise looked in my direction briefly as she and the King passed me by. She turned her head away as I tried to speak to her.

Bowen held back his horse to join me. We rode together, listening to the others talk.

"What did you say?" I asked after a while.

"We ride home," he said with a smile.

I gave a tired nod of understanding as he moved to the front of our group. The voices quieted down as he took his place and, with the lifting of his hand, as with each group before, we turned west. The morning sun warmed our backs, as I rolled the words lazily over in my mind...

"We ride home."

Chapter 11

I lost track of time. I only knew that when we stopped, I slept. I slept like the dead and upon waking, ate like it was my first time. Although we were no longer running for our lives, Bowen still held an agenda.

As we rode, the ground began to rise, changing again, becoming strewn with larger, roundish rocks. As we entered the foothills, mountains, rounded with time and weather, loomed ahead. Trees began to appear as we rode higher, becoming larger and larger, towers of shade and dark bark.

We threaded our way through the enormous trees, following some unseen path, ever higher into the mountains. Eventually the trail widened out, becoming better used, more visible to my untrained eye.

The horses sped up of their own volition toward a goal they knew to be close at hand. And then, from the trees, from the rocks, seemly from everywhere, came the sound of wild birds. The sounds I had come to know as the secret voices of the Jonda.

"Come, Brothers. Tonight we sleep in the arms of love," one of the Jonda cried and galloped ahead.

From behind the trees, several children ran in front of our caravan, heralding our arrival. Jonda of every age, size and description stood along the side of the trail to silently gawk at us. The village lay over the next rise, nestled in the bottom of a long, narrow valley. At long last, we had arrived.

I had never seen buildings of their kind in all my travels. Made of fallen trees and mud, they managed to blend into the surrounding forest. From the outside, the walls disappeared into the distance, obscured by smoke, people and trees. As best I could count, there were twenty of these structures, perhaps more. An intricate web of wide, dirt pathways laced them all together. Clouds of white smoke billowed from the center of each, filling the air with the aroma of cooking food and wood smoke.

We were lifted from our horses and swept inside the nearest structure. My head swam with new sights, sounds and smells as huge hands gripped me, handing me to the next and the next. Eloise squealed her protest as she and the King were lifted and passed, hand to hand to stand next to me at the center of the Jonda.

Inside, the walls were surprisingly smooth, almost white in color, which grew deeper with smoke stains the higher they raised, reaching a murky darkness in the upper timbers. Clay pots, alive with their own fire, hung from the walls, lighting the enormous hall.

Jonda, seemly hundreds of them, poured in behind us, forming a great, cheering circle about us. Eloise stood close behind me, clutching my shoulder.

"Bowen," a woman's voice called from deep within the mob. Pushing their way to the front, two women approached with Spath in tow.

"Spath's true love and her sister," Bowen whispered to me. "Nez," he yelled and ran to her outstretched arms.

She slipped her arm around him and they swung about the cavernous room from one end to the other as if involved in some grand dance. His voice rose and fell with great excitement as he greeted all those gathered there. His excitement was contagious and the crowd cheered with him.

"Cayra, Brothers, Cayra," Bowen yelled.

The crowd went wild with jubilation, filling the huge space with cheering voices, and the sounds of flutes and drums.

"Friends," Bowen called, raising his free hand into the air to quiet the crowd. "Friends," he repeated.

Slowly, the bedlam diminished.

He began to speak in Jonda as the circle about him widened. Many sat on the dirt floor. He walked the full circle as he spoke. His arms gestured with the action of his voice. He was story-telling, bringing all those present to understanding of the last few days. He pulled Spath to his feet to stand by him. He placed his hand on his shoulder and swept the air with the other, running the width of the room and ended pointing at me. The crowd cheered wildly, all eyes now fixed on me.

Bowen inflated his chest, sticking it out artificially. With his elbows cocked out from his side, he paraded around the circle with large comical steps. Spath followed close behind, mimicking his every move.

"I am Littlefield, keeper of Souls, friend of the Jonda. I come for the Truth sayer," he intoned in a mock voice. He suddenly crouched and slowly ran his hand from left to right in the air, speaking softly in Jonda once more.

There was a collective gasp from all present and then silence. Slowly, he stood up, turning his head from left to right. Spath followed his lead, standing; he pressed his back to Bowen.

"Norha!" his voice rang out with this one word. The word came from the back of his throat, low, husky, wet and carried a level of disdain.

A rush of excited and angry voices filled the chamber. Spath walked the circle, softly waving his hands to quiet the crowd. Bowen stood in the center, his head bowed. Eventually the silence returned.

"Come Soul Walkers," he started again. "Come She who Hunts. Tucker holds no fear, Tucker comes for Brother of the Sun, the Truth Sayer. Let none stand in my anger," his voice boomed as he held his palm high.

The crowd cheered with his antics. Several people closest to me patted me firmly on the shoulder. I was embarrassed. As he went on, Spath raised his arm to hold an invisible rope, his leg cocked out to his side.

"Norha!" Bowen yelled, hunching himself over, his fingers curled like claws, and walked the circle.

The Jonda booed and threw small objects at him as he passed.

Spath, his arm up, his leg out, yawned, patting his mouth with his free hand. Bowen crept up behind him, suddenly lunging to grab the out-held leg. Hunched over, he pretended to gnaw on Spath's leg with great animation and furious growling.

Spath yawned, continuing to pat his mouth with disinterest.

Bowen growled loudly and gestured to the King, beckoning him to join in their story-telling.

The King strolled to the center of the circle.

Bowen raced, disappearing briefly and then reappeared to hand a stick to the King before returning to chew on Spath's leg.

Recounting all that had happened, his voice excited, his

actions mirroring the words rushing out of him until the King stepped forward and slipped the stick between Bowen's arm and side. Bowen fell to the floor, washed away in frenzied voices.

The circle collapsed the Jonda rushing to pat the King, Spath and Bowen himself with happy hands.

The sound of drums and flutes burst to life, mixing with the excited voices filling the air. Seemingly, everyone came to pat my shoulder or that of the King, or shake our forearms.

The older women reconstructed a smaller version of the circle and began to dance. Food appeared and a celebration was now well underway.

Spath, shoved in one direction and then pushed in another, navigated his way through the throng, appearing at my side.

Someone pushed a wooden cup into my hand, a very small wooden cup, not much more than a thimble. A dark, pleasant smelling liquid swirled in the bottom. Floating on this estuary of discovery lay a tiny flower with five blue petals. At its center, a small yellow dot of color.

I glanced to Spath's cup, a much larger cup with three flowers floating there.

"I can't help but notice," I said over the music and the voices, pointing between his cup and mine.

His expression shifted, his broad smile dropping for a moment, trying to understand my meaning. Slowly, his smile returned.

"You are still a child of the world, Citizen. First crawl then walk with men," he said, downing his drink in total. He nodded, lifting his cup, for me to follow his lead.

"Child of the world, my ass," I said harshly and downed the concoction, flower and all.

The liquid was warm as it slipped down my throat and thicker than I had first thought. My tongue tingled. The concoction burned softly in my stomach.

As I turned my attention to Spath, I realized I was grinning, a wide, madman type of grin. I couldn't break the smile enough to speak. I could only nod.

"Tard," Spath said, tapping the rim of his cup. He grinned in return and matched my nod.

"Again?" I asked with hope large in my heart.

"Not yet, Brother. Wait for the blossom," he said, slipping his arm around my shoulder.

"Blossom? You mean the flower?" I slurred.

"Blossom," he returned.

My mind pulled at his words and then the word took on meaning of its own. My skin began to prickle. Slowly at first, starting deep inside the muscles and then pushing its way to the surface, roiling under my skin like boiling water, until every square inch of flesh felt as if it would jump off my body of its own volition. It tingled beyond any experience of my life. My feet itched with the reaction, making it difficult to stand still. The feeling intensified, growing warmer and warmer... slowly expanding up my body like a wick soaking up water, until it reached my scalp. I smoothed my hand over my head, flattening the sensation into my hair before it could escape.

As the feeling faded, my vision and hearing became sharp, clear, and much more acute. Colors became brighter, more vivid. It was as if I had transcended to a higher level of perception. I was still nodding.

"Again?" I asked through a frozen smile.

Spath slapped me on the back and laughed.

We downed another and my awareness jumped to the next level as the "blossom" repeated itself, only much faster this time. By the third round, I was convinced I could walk up walls and certain I was speaking Jonda. The music, the food, the people all swirled together, becoming a blur of color and noise.

Across the enormous room, a woman stood all alone, staring in our direction.

"Who is that?" I asked lifting my cup in her direction.

"Saris, sister of my wife," Spath answered.

"She's been watching me. I think I should go say hello," I said.

"Brother," Spath said harshly, grabbing my arm.

I looked at him bewildered.

"For Jonda, one cannot talk to a single woman without a relative present."

"You're a relative, right? Come on. Let's say hello,"

"You are a brave man, Brother. This is a danger I cannot allow," Bowen said, suddenly by our side.

He and Spath exchanged a few short angry words.

I walked away and left them to their discussion. I took aim and found my way across to Saris.

She was very pretty, as much as her younger sister or any woman I had ever seen. She was as tall as any Jonda man and very shapely, very well proportioned. Her black hair was braided at the temples and pulled back to hold the remainder in place. She wore a soft, short sleeved leather tunic over a matching skirt, partially opened on both sides, exposing her upper thigh and leg. Her copper skin showed seductively in contrast from under the cream-colored material. A curious braided leather belt hung loosely around her waist, strung within it, a round, red stone. It embellished her look... she was beautiful.

She pulled herself up straighter, rubbing her palms repeatedly over her hips. Her eyes were a deep, intense brown, with long desirable lashes.

"Hi, I'm Tucker," I said softly in my best Jonda.

She smiled at me shyly, but her body betrayed her. She shifted her weight, swaying with eager anticipation. She said nothing in response but looked anxiously about the room. I tried to get her to look at me but to no avail. She turned her head, looking past me as if searching for someone, becoming more and more anxious. At last, she crouched slightly and waved frantically. Her sister Nez made her way through the crowd to join us. Saris straightened, a large smile replacing the harried look on her face.

"Hi, I'm... " I started.

"Everyone here knows who you are," Nez said with a level of excitement.

I smiled with a slight nod.

"This is my sister Saris," she said with pride.

"Hi," I repeated, with a large smile.

Saris held her hands behind her back, swinging her shoulders back and forth shyly.

"It is our custom that I stay," Nez said, lowering her eyes.

"Sure. I understand," I said, leaning with my right hand against the wall. Nez looked to her sister who nodded her agreement.

She folded her arms and turned her back to us, remaining

in place. I smiled, soaking in her pretty face, trying to think of the right thing to say.

"Do you speak common?" I asked, not caring.

"Yes. Sister teach Saris good," she gushed, placing her hand on her sister's shoulder.

Nez didn't turn around but leaned her body back and forth to show her agreement.

"Husband Littlefield," Eloise's voice called out as she rushed to join us.

"Husband?" the sisters said at the same time, the irritation very clear in their voice.

"No, no, no, it's not what you think. She's not, I promise you. It's a joke, it's..." I stammered.

"Husband, who are these lovely people?" Eloise asked, slipping her arm around my waist. I tried to pull away, but only slightly.

The sisters glared at me, if looks could kill. My mind raced.

"This is Spath's wife Nez and her sister Saris," I said, trying to slip free of Eloise's grip.

"So happy to meet you, I am Eloise, the King's Governess," she said, offering her hand. Each of the sisters took her hand in turn. Both eyed her with more than mistrust.

"Husband, I think you've had enough to drink," she chided and pulled the tiny cup from my hand.

"She didn't mean it. She only said husband to... she's just trying to get my goat," I said apologetically.

Saris stepped closer, first eyeing me and then Eloise. Her face twisted into deep thought.

"Give back goat," she said, and pushed firmly against Eloise's shoulder.

I laughed. I know I shouldn't have but I couldn't help myself.

Eloise flushed a bright red with embarrassment. Speechless, she turned to walk away.

A smile of satisfaction passed between the sisters and Nez turned her back to us once more.

"Yes, you speak common very well," I said, wiping the tears of laughter from my eyes.

"Yes. Sister teach good."

"Yes, I would agree," I said smiling.

She looked about the room and then looked me over in detail, moving closer.

"Good hips," she said softly.

"I beg your pardon?"

"Tucker see Saris pretty, yes?" she asked.

"Yes, very pretty," I agreed, now seeing her in a new light.

"Good hips," she said, smoothing the palm of her hands down her thighs repeatedly.

"Oh yes," I agreed quickly. They were very good hips, indeed. A level of passion began to rise in me.

"Saris make good sons. Make many for Tucker," she said, moving closer to me, moving her leg through the slit in her skirt to touch my leg.

My heart jumped. As much as I wanted to finish this conversation I knew where it led. I began to pull away.

Her hand came out to me as if to keep me from leaving.

"Saris." I reached out in kind and gripped her forearm. "You are a very beautiful, very desirable woman and as much as I would like to continue this, I really must go," I said.

She squealed an ear-shattering squeal, gripping my arm all the tighter. Nez spun around. For a brief moment our eyes met and then she too shrieked and placed her hands on ours. Both jumped up and down with excited yells of glee. Their screams drew everyone's attention. They jumped up and down and spoke in excited rushes of Jonda. Saris refused to let go of my arm. Their words, their excitement, were contagious and quickly spread to the others.

I pulled desperately at her to free myself.

"What did you do?" Eloise asked angrily, suddenly by my side.

Spath and Bowen appeared as well. Their faces were a study of shock. Spath held a broad grin and joined in the jubilation.

"What did you do?" Eloise repeated, yanking me around to face her.

I was confused. Everyone was jumping and yelling at the same time.

"I didn't do anything, I swear," I yelled over the noise.

She looked deep into my face as if searching for a lie and then turned her glare to Bowen.

He flinched.

"Well?" she growled.

"He has asked Saris to marry him," he said, looking me straight in the face.

"What?" Eloise and I said at the same time.

"I didn't... I... I didn't say a word, I swear," I stammered.

"You held her arm," he said flatly.

My mind swirled. It was all happening too fast.

"I don't understand," I mouthed weakly.

"This," he said, grabbing my forearm as he had a hundred times before and squeezed tightly, "between men is friendship, a sign of respect between brothers. This between a man and woman is love... a contract."

"I didn't know." I yanked my arm away from him in shock. "I swear, I didn't know," I protested.

Eloise seethed, her nostrils flared, her eyes burned holes through me, glaring at me and then to the sisters.

"After all you've said to me, holding me, kissing me," she screamed and then slapped me hard.

Saris looked to me, then to Eloise, trying to understand. She turned to Nez, speaking in Jonda. Their words sped up quickly; it appeared our argument had passed to them.

Shortly, it passed to the others closest to us. It was growing, becoming worse. It appeared they were dividing into sides. Neither, however, regarded me with favor. I was stuck in the middle and looked to Bowen for a remedy. He pressed the palm of his hand against his forehead and melted back into the crowd. Over his disappearing shoulder, I caught a fleeting glimpse of Spath. He turned his head away quickly and vanished with Bowen.

"Hold," a deep voice called.

Two Jonda men dressed only in loincloths pressed their way through the crowd to stand at the center of the turmoil. Their bodies, all save their face, were covered with misshapen circles, painted with thin, dull yellow lines, making their copper skin look like turtle shells. Their hair hung in limp, wet, stringy strands to the middle of their chest. White shells strung in a row hung loosely about their necks.

All present bowed slightly, stepping aside in their passing silence filling the hole behind them. Nez spoke to them, pointing first at Eloise and then to Saris and finally to me.

My Jonda abilities failed me. I had no idea what they were saying.

The two men swung their heads from left to right as those about us voiced their agreement. The taller of the two spoke in loud sweeping tones, waving his hand in dismissal.

Nez tugged at Saris, trying to get her to leave. Saris reached out to grab my arm and pulled in return. Eloise suddenly grabbed the other and pulled me in the opposite direction. The crowd exploded into chaos again as I was sawed back and forth between them.

"Hold," the larger of the two "turtle" men called. They stepped between the women, freeing me from their grip.

"Saris want Tucker," Saris yelled and grabbed me by the back of the neck. "Saris be second wife."

All motion, all sound stopped. Everyone, especially me, was stunned.

"What did she say?" Eloise spoke first.

My mind had not returned from the whirlpool of panic streaming through it. I couldn't speak.

"Saris make good wife, second wife, after old wife," she continued.

"What did she say?" Eloise asked again, anger burning in her face. She pressed her body against me as if I held her from reaching Saris.

"Saris say, you first wife, old, dry, no sons. Die soon. Saris second wife, can wait, young, good hips, lots of sons. Live long time," she bellowed and pressed against me as well. "Many, many sons," she whispered into my ear, running her fingers through the hair at the back of my head. She pressed her body softly against mine and slipped her other hand inside my coat to smooth her hand over my chest.

I was flabbergasted.

The turtle man held up his hand, speaking in Jonda and the crowd nodded their agreement and slowly began to break up.

Saris didn't let go, nor did Eloise.

"We go to Daneba," the turtle man commanded, roughly pulling me free of the women.

The two men marched me out of the structure, the remainder of the Jonda followed.

"Daneba." It just kept getting better and better.

Chapter 12

The turtle men, one in front, one behind, led me through a maze of dirt paths deeper into the woods. Eloise and Saris stepped quickly behind with a large majority of the Jonda in tow behind them, at the head of them all Nez.

Bowen and Spath kept pace close behind her, arguing between themselves.

The dirt path narrowed, wandering uphill slightly, becoming less well worn. At the top of a small rise the ground leveled out, becoming a clearing among the huge trees.

A circle of nine large white stones about ten feet apart, taller than a Jonda, each buried to hold it on end, stood guardian in this place. Each had been hand carved to resemble the others. Each, however, held a different symbol carved into its face, pointing toward the center.

Two monoliths, one to each side of the path, stood slightly taller than the others. The turtle men and I stood at this entrance. The Jonda that followed lined themselves around the outside of the stone circle.

At the center of these stone guardians was a modest patchwork structure made from layers of overlapped animal skins stretched out on bent sticks. To the right of the shelter a fire jumped and danced, heating three perfectly round blue stones, each about twice the size of a Jonda's fist.

We stood silent for a moment, as if we were waiting for something. Eloise and Saris clung, one to each side of me, quietly placing themselves between the turtle men and me. I looked about at the faces of the Jonda encircling the stone barrier. All were serious, focused on the entrance to the animal skinned shelter. Shortly, the older women, having made their way to the front, began to chant in a low whispering rhythm, followed by the hollow, haunting sound of a single flute. We waited.

Someone moved inside the structure. The flap of animal skin that made up the door was flung open. Clouds of steam billowed out as if a great fire-breathing monster lay beyond the fur walls and had exhaled a long held breath.

Through the roiling mass a figure suddenly appeared as if deposited there by the vapor itself. As it began to thin the figure became clear.

Daneba.

She stood just outside the opening, her long black hair wet and stringy from the steam. An irregular shaped translucent green stone, wrapped with a silver wire, hung loosely around her neck. Her body, lean, muscular and naked from head to toe, dripped heavily from sweat from the steam. Her breasts hung slightly from age wet from the torrents of dripping sweat gliding over them. Her skin looked embattled, scarred. More than a third of the skin covering her chest appeared burnt, for lack of a better word... melted. Ridges of white flesh, frozen in distorted swirls marked her copper skin. On her arms and legs several large oval scars marred her body.

My heart jumped a little. They were slight, hollow gouges, dug into her muscle. I recognized them. They matched mine. She was no stranger to the Norha.

I had not realized how attractive a woman she was at our first meeting. Her eyes locked on me at the very moment the thought entered my mind. Without breaking eye contact with me, she raised her hand, gesturing to the others, and the chanting stopped. She stood unaware or uncaring of her nudity. Nor, it seemed, did anyone. No one so much as flinched or showed any sign of acknowledgment. For a moment her eyes left mine as she nodded to the lead turtle man.

He spoke in soft tones of Jonda as he gestured to the two women at my side. When he had finished she looked to the second for confirmation. He spoke in the same tones but gestured to the outer ring of people. She turned her head as if to memorize the faces of all present for some future retribution and then fixed her eyes on me once more. She shook her head slightly.

She said something in Jonda and a cheer went up from all present. Saris jumped into the air with a yelp of glee and planted a wet kiss on my cheek before filing off back the way we had come along with the others.

"What did she say?" Eloise asked harshly, turning me to face her.

"She said, fortune smiles on the man with two wives," the turtle man intoned, pushing past us. The two turtle men returned to the fire to stir it to greater height. Only Eloise and I were left standing at the stone portal.

"Look at what you've done," she yelled angrily.

"I didn't." The words were knocked from my mouth as she slapped me with all her might.

She stormed off, angrily talking to herself.

I rubbed my face, trying to get the feeling to return. I turned to Daneba who lifted her chin toward Eloise. I glanced back just as she pitched a rock at me. I lifted my feet in a jig like manner to escape its rolling assault. I bent to retrieve it. I had all intention of returning it to its sender.

Eloise bent at the waist, her hand and finger stretched to their limit, wagging, pointing at me.

"Don't you dare," she spit through clenched teeth I dropped the rock and showed her my empty hands.

She spun furiously and disappeared along the path, still talking to herself. Her muttering curses made wake as she continued down the trail back to the village. The whir of a stone hurled in my general direction as it tore through the low branches punctuated her words. I waited for a few moments until I thought it safe to follow.

"Citizen," Daneba called as I ventured to leave the safety of this place.

I turned to face her.

"Come inside. We have much to say," she said, before returning to the structure.

I hesitated. The turtle men flexed their fingers, popping their knuckles, eyeing me with anticipation.

I drew a deep breath of resignation and entered the stone circle. Immediately, I felt different. The air held the smell of fresh rain. The hairs on my arm stood up on end. I approached the hut, the flap now closed. As I tried to make up my mind, the flap was suddenly thrown open and I was bathed in white clouds of steam, Daneba's head the only thing visible to me.

"This is a sacred place, Citizen. Take off your clothes," she barked as if this were knowledge I possessed and defied.

I was not happy at the thought. I turned to leave. The turtle men were suddenly there to block my departure. I wasn't sure of what to do. Both men approached and began pulling at my clothes.

"Hang on, hang on. I'll do it," I said shoving at their hands.

They waited, arms folded as I took off my clothes... all save my under garments.

"All." The turtle men said in unison, leaning forward to menace me into submission.

I turned my back to them and pulled the last of my clothes from my body and handed it to them. They took them along with what little I have to pass for dignity. I stood with my back to them and covered myself. One of them poked me in the side. In his hand lay a piece of leather, attached to it, a string of red rope. It was a loincloth. I placed it quickly about my waist hanging in front, a large uneven square, in back a smaller one.

"Aaghh," one of the turtle men cried and yanked the rope, spinning it around my waist, placing the small one in front and the large one in back.

"It's my first time," I offered weakly.

The turtle men said nothing, only pointed to the hut.

I followed their direction and lifted the flap. Again, I was assaulted with billowing steam. I slipped in as best I could, pushing against the hot air trying to escape.

Inside, the walls were the same patchwork of skins held up on a skeleton of willow branches. The floor was packed dirt and sloped to the center slightly. Placed at the heart of all this sat an iron basket on three small legs.

Held in its grip were six green stones. The air was thick with moisture, very hot and hard to breathe. Sweat jumped to the surface of my skin, instantly drenching me.

One of the turtle men pushed his way inside with a forked branch, forcing me deeper into the heat. He had fished one of the hot stones from the fire outside, depositing it into the iron basket with the others before disappearing behind the flap.

"Sit."

On the opposite side Daneba sat, cross-legged, next to a bucket. She drew a large wooden ladle from the receptacle, scooping water from it to pour over the hot rocks in the iron basket. Steam exploded into the air, with a loud hiss. The temperature rose with the new addition.

I looked about, trying to find a comfortable place to sit down.

"Here," she scolded and patted the dirt next to her.

I glued my eyes to the ground, making my way across the small chamber. If I didn't look at her nakedness she wouldn't look at mine, or so I hoped. Sitting down in a loincloth was more problematic than I would have thought.

I managed with a minimum of embarrassment.

"It looks good on you," she said, watching me with great interest and a large smile. She was enjoying my discomfort.

"Stop it," I said.

She just smiled and poured more water on the rocks, creating more heat, making the air heavier, wetter, and more difficult to breathe.

"About Saris. I didn't."

"I'll talk to her. Hold no doubt," she said, pouring more water.

She called out in Jonda to the turtle men. Almost immediately one of them entered carrying an ocean shell. Rough, ugly and well used on its exterior, its polished interior shone with various shades of blue and silver. It was large enough to be a bowl. He held it with two hands and presented it with a slight bow. In its modest depth something burned. It was pungent, overpowering. Wisps of dull gray smoke lazily drifted out of its heart.

Daneba took the shell, placing it on the ground in front of her. Inside several strands of a pale green dried herb had been tied together with red thread, forming a bundle as thick as a man's thumb. She scooped the smoke midair with cupped hands, coaxing it over her body.

"What is it?" I asked, more than a little concerned.

"Sage," she said, lifting the shell. She removed the smoldering bundle and waved it like a wand, washing the smoke over me, muttering a prayer before setting it aside. "It is the psychical soul of the world itself. It will guard us from evil. It frees the truth, in us both."

We sat quietly for awhile as sweat poured out of me. One of the turtle men came in with another stone. It was barely settled in its cradle when Daneba emptied the contents from her ladle once more.

"Why are we here?" I gasped, trying to place the small

square of leather in a strategic correct place.

"We are here to see what there is to see," she said, closing her eyes.

"I don't understand," I said, wiping the sweat from my face.

"I'm surprised to see you alive, Citizen," she said flatly, without looking at me.

"Frankly, so am I," I responded, tugging at the loincloth.

"It's my fault," her words trailed off.

"What is?" I asked, squirming in the heat.

"All of it, you, Enon, the Norha, even Kathryn I suppose."

"Enon? The Norha?" I asked, straining to make my mind work under the heat. "Shouldn't we be doing something to find Elizabeth?"

"She's safe, for now," she announced flatly and poured more water.

"How can you be sure?"

"No harm will come to her. If Kathryn wanted her dead, she never would have left her mother's arms. She has much larger plans for Elizabeth."

I turned the thought over in my mind. My head swam. I was becoming light headed, dizzy, from the heat, almost delusional. I struggled to put a thought together.

"Larger plans? How do you know? How is it your fault? And what about Enon?"

Her eyes flashed angrily. For a moment her face hardened, twisting into a mixture of hesitation and, perhaps... hate.

"You see these burns?" she asked through clenched teeth, pointing at her chest.

"Yes," I said, not wanting to look.

"This is the price of desire, the price of arrogance and all the promise it holds." Her voice suddenly weakening, trailing off. "Kathryn was my pupil. I taught her all I had to teach. I created her, allowing her to become the monster she is today," she whispered shamefully.

"What the hell were you trying to do?" The words jumped out of my mouth without the filter of good sense.

"There are things beyond imagining, Citizen, and the pursuit can be intoxicating and you will do anything... anything... to obtain it. Even the torture of a little girl's body and soul and Kathryn was an apt student... too apt," she said, her eyes fixed on me. Something in her tone chilled me. Her face held a frightening scowl, as if she were waiting for a reaction, some form of disdain to show on my part.

"And Enon?" I asked, trying to change the subject.

"Enon has been the last thread tying me to the people, the last virtue that protected me from myself, to pull me back to the Goddess. Kathryn's taking of Elizabeth is her twisted sense of justice. She will gain what I could not and punishes me and the child's father all in one foul act. She will use the child as I had used her," she said defiantly, pulling back her shoulders, straightening her spine, waiting for my reaction.

"Enon is Elizabeth's father?" I was rocked. My mind spun under the thought. "Does she know?"

"I'm sure Kathryn has made certain of it by now."

"How do you know?" I asked my mind moved sluggishly.

"It's enough that I know, Citizen," she said, turning her head to face me. "Enon's sorrows are my fault. I didn't trust his judgment, I didn't trust you."

My mind swirled too much to form an answer.

"I have the chance to make it right, Citizen," she said and pushed me over lightly.

I stretched out across the ground, trying to pull all the cool moisture the soil had to offer into my body.

"I should have let you die," she said, suddenly shifting her body, kneeling over me on all fours.

My mind swirled. I wanted to lift my arms to push her away, but couldn't. The heat, the steam, the tard drained me of all strength, of all will.

She moved almost liquid in manner, to stand over me, only half-visible through the steam. Her voice called out in Jonda and the turtle men appeared. They scooped me up between them; my arms but limp offshoots of weakened flesh thrown over their shoulders. We followed her outside.

Instantly, my body was drenched in cold air. I thought I could hear the sweat covering my body turn to ice.

The turtle men dragged me to the fire and dropped me to the ground like a bag of rocks. I lay helpless, struggling to look about as the turtle men and Daneba disappeared from view.

Time passed slowly; eventually they returned.

They carried someone else bundled in a white robe. They brought their charge close to the fire and laid it gently on the ground. A moment later they reappeared with a second. Smaller than the first, it squirmed to be released but failed in its attempt to free itself from its wrappings.

The turtle men stirred the fire to new heights as Daneba reappeared. She wore a blue robe of transparent material that did little to cover her nudity. Her black hair now held a complex braid, woven within it, several silver metal objects. She nodded toward the men and each moved to uncover their bundles.

The first, Enon, unconscious and nude as well, lay on the opposite side of the fire. The second bundle, Noget, Enon's dog.

"I had thought him dead," I said half aloud, half to myself, as the dog's head turned weakly to stare at me. I was overwhelmed with a mixture of surprise, pleasure and fear.

"As I had you, Citizen," Daneba said.

I tried to roll over, to get up. One of the turtle men pressed his foot into my chest, pinning me to the ground. The second threw an armful of wood on the fire and it jumped to life in a most unnatural way. I was instantly covered in a shower of sparks. I pushed to free myself from the turtle man's heel, managing to sit up.

"Oh no, Citizen, not this time. This time," she hissed, shoving me to the ground with her foot. "This time I want you to remember everything. I will make sure you never forget this day or my words."

The turtle men began a low, soft chant, encouraging the flames to vault ever higher. Daneba's voice suddenly joined in louder, fuller than theirs. The flames roared, exploding with heat pressing against my naked flesh. I tried to scramble to my feet, to escape at any cost.

At Daneba's bidding, the flames reached out for me, driving itself into the ground, splashing like fingers of water, blocking my escape. At every turn the flames snaked itself in front of me, becoming ever larger and forming a broad circle about us. The symbols carved into the stone began glow a brilliant blue, holding the flames in check.

Many of the Jonda had returned, prodded either by the chanting of the turtle men or the roar of the flames. I rushed with weakened limbs to the stone portal. Beyond the yellow curtain of flames stood Eloise, the image of her worried face danced and vanished to reappear through the fingers of heat at another part of the ring. The voices of those on the other side were muddled, indistinguishable, washed away in the roar of flames that now climbed to the sky itself, holding me in and all others out.

At the center of this mayhem, the flames spun, thick as tree limbs, twisting around itself, climbing upon itself, a whirlwind of conflagration.

Daneba called out and the fire bent to her bidding. It shifted at its middle, appearing more alive than mere flames, bowing to her, growing ever larger. Her voice reached a wild, crazed pitch, as lightning sprang from her hand. It leapt into the heart of the twisting braids of fire and with a blast of sound that drove me to the ground, it broke them apart. The writhing column of fire shattered into three pieces, spinning independently of each other.

The first, the one closest to Daneba, expanded wildly, becoming more solid in appearance before moving to consume Enon. I stared in horror as it slid over him, devouring all sight of him.

Daneba stood before it and as she raised her hand it flexed, pushing closer to the ground and Enon reappeared, forced to the top, pushed up through its very center. The flames pulled at him, spreading his limp body out over its mass. His arms hung lifeless at his side. His spine curved back, arching his naked body over the fountainhead of flames, all but folding him backward, yet he remained unharmed, untouched by the flames. For all outward appearances, he was dead. His body, washed within the flames, bobbed up and down slowly as if drifting upon swells of water. His copper skin was pale, his face lifeless. For a moment, as his body spun in my direction, his eyes half opened.

A chill rushed over me; my skin rippled with goose bumps.

"Cayra, brother," The words slipped from his lips as if whispered from beyond the grave.

I scrambled to escape, seeking a weakness in the curtain, but none was to be found.

"Citizen," Daneba's voice pierced the roar of the fire.

I spun to face her.

She reached out, extending her hand toward me. Instantly, thunder boomed and a blinding bolt of lightning sprang from her hand.

It lashed out, burying itself deep into my chest, lifting me off the ground. I reeled in shocking pain. I screamed from the bottom of my lungs, pulling my last breath through a rasping throat before falling to the ground. I pushed against the hot dirt on all fours.

"You've gone mad," I accused. My words burned in my throat as I gasped for air.

"Not mad enough, Citizen. We've only just begun," she said through clenched teeth.

I struggled to stand. My chest ached, my skin slightly charred. I staggered under the thought of perishing at the hand of this deranged woman.

The second fire column spun toward me. I covered my face with my arms, resigning myself to my fate. Its heat pushed at me. My head swam. The roar from the swirling flames was deafening, drowning out the words Daneba and the turtle men chanted.

The flames shifted, mutated, forming a hollow to surround me. I closed my eyes as tiny hand and arm like appendages appeared from the walls to grasp at me.

I was lifted, pushed through the column to the top just as Enon had been. I was held, stretched helplessly backward over the top of the flames, undulating softly up and down. I fought to remain conscious.

The dog was next, lifted by the remaining column as Enon and I had been, rendered as lifeless.

"I have seen the future, Citizen. Yours will not be an easy path to follow. The fate of the Jonda will depend on your choices. You will have sacrifice and heart break. Remember my words, Citizen. Never reach out in anger. Use your endowment wisely. A horrible death lives within you. Remember my words," she screamed over the roar of flames.

The flames turned me to face her and then rotated Enon and the dog as well. Daneba stepped into the center of the flames, raising both hands. Lightning sprang from her, pounding into my chest once more. It leapt from me to Enon and then to the dog. I screamed for all I was worth but couldn't move or free myself. The lightning poured into me, filling every fiber of my body, wracking me with incredible pain. It enveloped me, all but stopping my heart. It shifted, sizzled, and burned into me before changing color, becoming a deep blue. As it did so I was washed away with thoughts, memories and experiences not my own.

My life, all that I had done, every meal, every thought, every woman I had ever known, all came to life for me once more, mixing with those of the dog and of Enon. His mind, the dog's all spun together becoming one thought, one life.

There was no line of distinction between any. I no longer knew where I left off and Enon, or the dog for that matter, began.

For a moment my mind was awash with images of Daneba herself. It was as if I were seeing the world through her eyes rather than mine.

The first image, lightning sprang from her hand. She stood outside a circle of blue flames, sending bolt after massive bolt, sizzling through the air.

The picture spun and swirled like water in my mind, dissolving and reassembling again. From within the circle an equal amount of energy was being returned. My heart pounded wildly, threatening to jump out of my chest as the image increased in clarity, becoming more real, more intense. For a fleeting moment the heart of this madness was revealed. From deep within the depths of blue flames, a blistering ball of fire was flung toward Daneba. A second and then a third, each larger than the one before, burned through the air as they sought their target, the image of Daneba lying on the ground, defeated, her body ablaze swam through my head. It swirled briefly and then was replaced by her vanquisher. My heart pumped with true fear, as the image became clear...

Kathryn. The jolt of her face brought me back to consciousness and I was awake again.

Time stood still within this hell. As I stared in disbelief, fingers of flame pulled open my chest, exposing my beating heart. Enon and the dog quickly followed suit and a bright orange spark of energy jumped between us connecting all at the same time. The sound of the flames, her voice, all mixed with the swirl of images saturating my mind, becoming too much for me to bear.

As I moved toward unconsciousness or perhaps death itself, Daneba sent another burst of lightning into my chest. It poured through every fiber of me.

I had no anguish left to feel, no power left in me to scream. If it meant escape from the pain, I welcomed it. At last, I could take no more. I gave into fate and allowed the pain to overtake me. The images pounding in my head slowed, dividing themselves into groups, and then slowly faded away until, at last, all I could remember were mine alone.

Something, however, was different. Something was left behind by the images. I felt as though all the ancestors that stood behind Enon now stood behind me as well.

I felt, for the first time in my life, a sense of family... part of a larger whole, more than a citizen... the next in a long line... a Jonda.

Chapter 13

My eyelids felt too heavy to open and I was freezing. My arms and legs, stretched to their fullest, refused to move. I was wet, cold and, for a moment, certain I was dead.

I was naked, tucked inside an animal skin. The fur had been turned to the inside and I had been sown between its layers. My head was pointing upstream. Water rushed over me, threatening to drown me. My teeth chattered and I struggled to turn my head. I was pushed under the water and floated to the top again and again.

I thrashed about trying to pull my head free of the water, to right myself but could not. Only then did I realize I was tied. A rope, tied to nearby trees, held each limb outstretched, suspending me in the middle of a rushing stream.

"Goddess," I cursed.

"Governess, our little fish is awake," the King's voice gurgled as my head bobbed in and out of the water.

"Help me," I cried as my head rose briefly.

"Husband not worry, safe now, Saris tied good." Her words filtered through the water clogging my ears.

"I've never seen you look better, Mr. Littlefield," Eloise chided. She stood on the bank with a smug look on her face. She folded her arms and gloated with satisfaction.

Bowen and Spath untied the ropes holding my feet and they sank like a stone. The water pulled at me, threatening to wash me downstream. I struggled to get to my feet, my arms still tied outstretched. The water washed me off my feet and I was dunked once more.

Bowen and Spath ran to untie me. Spath cut the rope freeing me, letting my arm drop to my side. Bowen was slower, taking his time to untie the rope. I pulled slightly against it to stay upright. As he finally untied it, he pulled it hard. I stumbled forward and was washed under the water again. He held the rope taunt, his feet spread wide. Something in his face was dark, brooding.

He just stood there. I flopped around, splashing wildly and cursed.

Suddenly a loud crack snapped in the air. The leather belt wrapped about Saris's waist was in actuality a whip. She reached out toward Bowen and cracked it again.

They began to argue hotly in Jonda and Bowen yanked the rope again, pulling me deeper into the water. Saris cracked the whip a third time and Bowen let go, throwing the rope toward me.

My fur cocoon became heavier as I struggled to escape the water. The King and Spath stepped into the stream to help me out of my dilemma.

Back on shore, I was cut free of ropes as well as the fur. I stood naked, covered only in goose bumps.

My body, burnt a deep red, was covered with white blisters. I ran my hands over my aching torso. Carved into my flesh by Daneba's lightning, three large deep burns decorated my chest. Each a deep, putrid black and blue, formed a star with fingers radiating from its center, covering my chest like ghastly webs. Through the center of the purple fingers, a line of black flesh held the majority of pain.

"All look. Saris husband fine. Three times Daneba touch. Three times husband Littlefield cheats death say this all Daneba's power? Have mosquito bites more trouble than this."

Wild voices in Jonda rose into a cheer.

As I looked about, half, if not all, of the village stood, watching my predicament. I wanted to cover myself, to hide my nudity, but it seemed pointless now.

An old woman approached, carrying a cup. She held it with two hands, being careful not to spill any of its contents. As she drew closer, she held it out to me. Still shaking from the cold water, I took it from her wrinkled hands.

She stood for a moment, looking me over. It took a moment for her eyes to return to mine. A sly smile crossed her lips and she looked down again before turning to leave.

In the cup, Tard, only with three flowers this time. I drank it without hesitation. As the bloom swept over my body, my pain subsided.

As it took root within me, the blisters covering my body began to disappear, my skin less red. The three stars and their fingers diminished considerably and my strength returned. I swirled the last of the liquid slightly before turning the cup upside down into my mouth, waiting for the last drop. Once empty, I thrust the cup over my head.

A tempestuous cheer from the Jonda came in response.

Saris moved to stand beside me. She placed one hand on my shoulder and held the coiled whip in the other. She smoothed her hand over my back.

"Many, many sons," she whispered to me, brushing her whip against my manhood.

Her breath in my ear sent shutters of excitement racing up my spine, faster than Daneba's lightening. I was surprised by my involuntary reaction.

"Put these on," Eloise said, pushing her way between us. "You're making a fool of yourself," she added brusquely, shoving my clothing at me.

I turned my back and began to slip them on. As I did so, Bowen bumped me with his hip in his passing, almost knocking me to the ground.

"Second wife," Saris called after him angrily.

Bowen walked away unaffected and uninterested.

"What the hell is his problem?" I asked Spath as I tried to adjust my pants.

"Second wife," he said, lifting his chin toward Saris.

I turned to look at her. Her nostrils flared, her chest heaved and her eyes burned holes into Bowen's back.

Eloise stood looking at me, at my nudity to be more exact, as I dressed.

"Are you done?" I asked with irritation, openly embarrassed.

"I can't imagine what you mean," she said and turned to follow Bowen.

I watched her walk away. Her hips swung with a hypnotic rhythm.

"Remember, Mr. Littlefield, first wife," she said, glancing over her shoulder to smile at me.

I followed her with my eyes for as long as I could see her.

Laughter from the King broke my concentration.

"What?" I asked.

"I didn't say a thing," he responded, holding up his hands as he followed her down the path.

All but alone, I got dressed and followed the others through the trees to the village.

I let my mind drift. Eloise and Saris; I played with the idea of two wives, imagining all the possibilities. The thought started out innocently enough, in fact exciting, but quickly became a nightmare. In a few fleeting moments of imagination, I saw a future controlled by not one but two wives, each competing for total control over me, neither happy with the influence of the other. I would never be out of their sight. Never free to enjoy a moment of peace. I shook the thought out of my head. I tried to force my mind to be blank. I didn't want those pictures in my head.

As the more pleasant aspect of two wives worked at the edges of my mind once more, someone was running to greet me.

A young man, speaking excitedly to me in Jonda grabbed my arm and pulled me frantically in an effort to make me follow him. We ran among the trees, racing toward the growing sound of voices ahead. I had difficulty keeping up with him.

There in a small clearing, many of the Jonda stood about, speaking in loud and angry voices.

Many of them shook their fist and kicked dirt.

At their center, two men, dressed only in loincloths, crouched close to the ground. Although similar to the Jonda, they appeared slightly smaller, squarer and squatter. Their noses were flat and broader, their face long and thin. Large arcs had been shaved into the hair at their temples and painted red with black detail. The design reached from cheekbone to the back of their heads, giving a horn like appearance.

Cuts and bruises of every size covered their bodies. Blood oozed openly from their wounds, painting their copper skin. Between them, a third, younger man lay on the ground, bleeding. His wounds were drastically worse. He moaned in great pain. A large portion of his upper leg was missing and bled profusely. The scars, the cuts and the missing flesh; all the blood could only mean one thing... the Norha.

"Who are they," I asked as Bowen turned toward me.

"They are the Jansu. Brother of the Norha." It was Daneba. She and the Turtlemen stood at the top of the rise, just beyond the clearing.

"The Norha?" I asked, turning to her.

"Stay clear, Citizen. There is still much you don't understand," she admonished.

"I have no desire to see the Norha again, or any of their relatives," I said with tension in my voice.

"Desire or not, they are not done with you," she said, pointing at me.

"Well, I'm done with them," I said flatly.

One of the young man's companions reached out for me, pulling me to them. He spoke in rushed words as he moved to one side to make room for me.

"I don't understand you," I said with panic.

"He says this is his younger brother," Bowen said solemnly. "He wants you to save him."

"Tell him I can't. I don't know how," I said, trying to stand.

The man pulled me down again and gave me a harsh look. His sibling, lifting his head with great effort, tried to speak. His words faint, all but lost as they slipped from his lips mixed with the blood oozing from his mouth. He spoke in words not Jonda, not Norha, but soft, easy words as he tried to turn his face toward me. His eyes met mine for a moment. A weak smile glided across his young face before he returned his gaze to his brother. Slowly, his eyes closed and his face went lax.

Bowen now stood next to me and placed a hand on my shoulder.

The two men hung their head briefly before looking to me. Their eyes were filled with their loss.

"I'm sorry," I said.

The brother's eyes hardened. He spoke in short, crisp words and then spit at the ground. They turned away from me.

"What did he say?" I asked Bowen urgently.

Bowen said nothing but flexed his fingers holding my shoulder.

"Tell me," I insisted.

"He says... You are a coward. You are no Soul-Bearer."

My heart sank with his words.

The two men removed a dagger from a leather sheath at their side and smeared it with their own blood.

My mind raced with uncertainty; my heart banged in my chest.

A sound, a gurgle, a moan, something drifted from the young man's body.

I stood slowly but Bowen blocked my retreat, his hand still firmly on my shoulder.

The two men crouched, their daggers poised over the body.

Under the flesh, something moved.

The men tensed, lifting their daggers to the ready.

My mind raced with that ugly sound. I struggled to pull free of Bowen's grip but could not. He held me rock solid.

The sound, the movement, grew louder, becoming more ferocious and a scrap of both entities had begun to appear. A soul walker was about to enter the world.

"No," I screamed and thrust my hand out to deny the reality as the two halves of the man's soul burst from his flesh.

The battle of supremacy had begun.

The sounds filled me with terror, sickening me. My stomach pitched, my innards squirmed within me.

My feet suddenly tingled and felt hot; energy pushed to flow through me. It was as if lightning were rising from the ground itself to enter my body. It pulsed from my feet and up my legs. For a moment, my knees shook, threatening to buckle under me. The energy accelerated to fill my body like water rushing to fill an empty vessel. It surged down my arm to my outstretched hand.

The emblems branded into my palm sprang to life with a dull yellow glow and flexed with incredible pain. I screamed a horrible scream from deep inside my soul. The symbols appeared to shift, to rotate.

They swirled, melting together, covering the entirety of my hand, becoming brighter and brighter.

I thrust my hand away, terrified of the transformation overtaking me. The energy grew rapidly, filling me to overflowing.

A white light, a fire of sorts, leapt from my hand. It crackled with a power, a purpose, and a life of its own.

The two bloodied men jumped to the side, escaping the touch of light as it burst from me. It washed over the young man lying on the ground, bathing him from head to toe. My stomach churned wildly. The energy flowed freely, coursing up from the center of the world, from its very soul.

It ran through me faster and faster, growing in volume and power. There was no stopping it. My hand shook violently and the air crackled with the power emanating from me.

The creatures, battling to become a soul walker, swirled through the air, unaware of my transformation.

The light poured over the body with an unexpected intensity. It began to dissolve like snow in a warm sun, slipping away moment by moment, melting into the soil until it was gone.

The two halves of his soul fought for domination over the other. Tangled within themselves, they fell within the scope of the light. Instantly, each abandoned their quest and sought escape from its touch. Neither could avoid the inevitable. They were pulled deeper into the light, forced together to become a single entity again.

Newly formed, it fought against the light with a threatened ferocity. Slowly it tired, turned, and then plunged into my chest. It hit me with force, driving me to the ground on all fours. The light pulsed briefly and then disappeared into my palm from which it came.

My stomach twisted into a knot. My mind spun, instantly filled with a tempest of rushing images. The young man's life, from beginning to end unfolded before me and then, like a dying ember, faded away.

I gasped for breath, turning my head to look at the brother. He and his companion were sprawled on their backs, trying to move away from me, pushing at the dirt with their heels, looking like crabs.

Bowen helped pull me to my feet, as I wobbled.

The two men rose. The brother approached me, eyeing me closely, and his dagger still in his hand. He stood motionless, his gaze locked on me. And then, without a word, he reached behind his head, pulling his hair forward. Tied in a bundle like the Jonda, he took a fist full of the hair and cut it. He hesitated for a moment and then thrust it out toward me. I took it with trepidation, clutching it tightly in my fist. He stared at me unblinking for a moment before giving me a quick nod. I did the same. He grabbed my forearm and squeezed tightly. Again, I followed his lead.

He let me go and turned to Bowen. They spoke in low,

soft words as they locked forearms. Both men glanced at me briefly. Their faces were unsettled. Their eyes spoke of concern, perhaps of fear. Their expressions cut me.

They dropped their eyes and turned a shoulder to me, continuing to speak. My heart flinched and I fought not to turn my face away.

"He says there are many Norha in the woods these days. There is much interest in the path of the Jonda," Bowen said, dividing his attention between the horned man and me.

"He says the Jansu follow the Dog of the Huntress," Bowen intoned, lifting his chin to me.

I didn't understand his meaning.

"The 'Dog' follows the child," he said rigidly.

"Grimwell," the King said, pushing his way to stand beside me.

Bowen nodded his agreement.

The Jonda argued loudly amongst themselves.

"Jansu say truth. Enon follow also," he shouted, his voice suddenly louder than the others.

I turned as Enon pushed past Daneba with a slight bow. Next to him strolled the dog. I was very happy to see him and, strangely, the dog as well.

A cheer, full of the desire for bloodletting, rose from the Jonda.

Three pronged stone clubs seemed to appear from nowhere as they howled and roared their excitement. The horned men pumped an arm up and down and tilted their heads back, barking like wild dogs, adding to the anxiety coursing through me.

The Jonda grew wilder in their excitement, behaving as the horned men did. The look on their faces chilled me and in them I saw the savages so many feared and with one last blood-curdling howl from the horned men, a new madness devouring them all. They ran headlong into the trees with Enon and the dog at the lead.

"Bowen," I said, grabbing his arm. "What if it's a trap?"

"Then we kill the Jansu and you eat their souls," he said roughly before disappearing into the trees after the others.

Saris slipped a gentle hand on my shoulder as the ferocious voices of the Jonda mixed with those of the horned men, almost becoming a chant.

I stood for a moment listening.

"What are they saying?" I asked, without turning to her.

"We follow the dog," she said softly.

"We follow the dog," the King repeated with ghoulish delight, brushing against me. He ran, sword in hand, swallowed within the same madness, into the trees after the others.

Chapter 14

It seemed as though the madness would never stop. Horned men and Jonda alike searched the forest for Norha. They killed them, all of them that could be found.

The Jansu took a great deal of delight in the taking of Norha hair. They carved it from their victim's skulls in wide swaths of bloody flesh, whether dead or alive. They were madmen, as horrible as any Norha.

The fire erupted from my hand again and again, rushing from me in torrents. It was a terrible weapon. Nothing stood before its touch.

It stripped flesh from bone and turned bone to dust. Soul upon soul, Jonda, Jansu and Norha alike found their way to me, filling and sickening me.

Slowly, with each new encounter I grew stronger in its control. The energy shifting within me felt different in its passing, and in doing so became a bright blue in color.

I was no longer a slave to its whim. I could change it, shape it, and make it do my bidding until at last, I could heal. As I passed my hand over the broken and bleeding bodies of the Jonda, their wounds buckled and rippled from within as if moving in reverse, knitting bone and flesh together to make them all but whole again.

I took those Norha souls with equal fervor to the lives I saved. I had become God and monster all in one.

Two days went by as we forged our way deeper into the mountains, leaving a trail of dead Norha in our wake.

The battles were too easily won. The number of Norha grew smaller in front of us and now, following our lead, larger behind us.

We were traveling deeper into their territory. The Jansu followed the Norha, the Norha followed Grimwell, Grimwell followed Kathryn, and she had the child. It didn't take long for the truth to show itself. We were being led to her, pushed from behind. Enon was blind to all but the path that led to Elizabeth.

On the morning of the third day, the Jansu, laden with

Norha trophies, turned to the East for home. They had had enough. Our numbers grew smaller as the day wore on. Cluster by cluster the Jonda did the same. By day's end, little more than Bowen, the King, my two wives and I followed Enon.

Day was becoming night.

Enon refused to stop. No food, no fire, no sleep.

What pulled at him, pulled also at me to a lesser degree. My body would not do all for me that he demanded of his, but I followed with all I had to give.

A sliver of moon burned a dull red as it crested. Under that light, the trees grew smaller until disappearing altogether, giving way to a hard, compact, lifeless dirt.

Our path rose steeper, becoming narrower. We formed a line, each stepping where those in front had stepped, finding our path... the dog.

The night seemed to go on forever.

Slowly, we climbed higher and higher until the cool night air was difficult to breathe. Soaked in sweat, my skin rippled with goose bumps.

At last we stopped. The ground rolled softly here, becoming almost flat, slightly wider than the path we had transverse.

"Rest now," Enon said and walked away.

No one said a word but simply collapsed to the ground, exhausted. I leaned against a broad rock and gladly closed my eyes. Eloise jostled to sit next to me, leaning her head on my shoulder. I smiled weakly and patted her hand, closing my eyes again. After a moment Saris crawled to the ground next to me and laid her head on my lap. I didn't care, nor did Eloise.

Sleep poured thick and heavy over us. After what seemed like only seconds, a warm morning sun awakened me. My body hungered for more rest. Silently, we were moving again.

We climbed ever higher as the day grew longer.

Below us, the constant thrum of the Roar of the Bear meant the Norha were close behind and still following. The rhythmic sound was unnerving.

Our path spiraled up the side of the mountain. We clung to its steep walls for fear of falling. No matter how high we climbed, the mountain towered ever higher above us, disappearing into the swirling clouds.

The dog, as brisk as ever, pushed by me to sniff the ground and then promptly pushed by again to return to the front of the line before disappearing behind a rock outcropping. All I wanted was to catch my breath and sit for just a little while, but neither Enon nor Eloise would have any of that.

"Dog say Izie here," Enon said.

"Here?" I asked, thinking he must have gone mad.

"Dog say this way," he said and ducked into an opening in the side of the mountain.

It appeared to be little more than a slit in the stone, barely wide enough for him. For a moment he was stuck. He jerked his body several times, forcing it to the opposite side. There, inside the opening in the stone, was an alcove of sorts, slightly wider than the entrance.

"Tucker come," he said, holding out his hand from the opening.

"In there? Are you out of your mind?" I asked, stepping well out of his reach.

"I'll go. If Elizabeth and Grimwell are in there, I'll go," the King said and, lighting a torch, pressed his body through to follow Enon.

Bowen pulled at Saris' arm, saying something in Jonda.

"Second wife," she snapped and reached out for me, pulling free of him.

He yanked his hand from her as if burnt and she the fire. He gave me an icy stare before following the King into the hole.

Eloise was next, slipping through with little effort.

Saris lit another torch and followed the rest.

"Husband," Eloise said softly, standing at the opening, her hand stretched out to me.

Framed by the opening in the stone, lit from behind by torches, she was compelling.

"Are you people crazy? Do you know what's in there?" I asked, stepping back a little more.

She stepped out, coming closer. Her face, now filled with all the anguish, all the hope that still lay ahead, was moist with tears.

"Elizabeth," she said quietly.

The word stabbed into my heart. Why couldn't they see? There was no air, nowhere to go and it was dark. It was like being buried alive.

"Husband," she repeated.

I turned my back to her, struggling, fighting the desire to escape, to be done with all of it. I hated myself but couldn't bring myself to go in there. How could I? How could they ask that of me?

I stood at the edge, looking out over the expanse of land before me. I could see for miles in every direction, save for the massive wall of stone that now lay at my back. Beyond this point, the landscape stretched out, becoming a line between the sky and the very end of the world. A dull reddish-brown hue, it became almost gray, like dead wood, at the far edges of its creation. As far as the eye could see, it was scarred with deep fingers of erosion that radiated its full length and breadth, punctuated only by tall, sharp hillocks. They looked as if they were formed by the keen-edged finger of a great demon, pushing up from underneath. No blade of grass, no bird, no living thing moved here. It was naked, stripped of all life.

A scattering of clouds drifted slowly overhead. Their shadows shifted and changed in size and shape. They glided together to become a larger, brooding mass and then floated away, becoming smaller shredded pieces of their former selves. They were a herd of dark things that slid over this broken land, searching for some form of solace.

Protected by the mountain, only the slightest of breezes moved here. The loneliness of this place, the heartbreaking silence, all tormented my soul.

"Husband," Eloise called softly, her hand beckoning to me.

"You don't know what you're asking of me," I said, wiping the tears burning my face.

"I do know, but Elizabeth needs us," she said, slipping closer, taking my hand.

"I can't."

"For Elizabeth... for me," she soothed, pulling me toward the opening.

I looked into those tearful eyes and the world of sanity

slowly drifted away. I nodded my agreement and followed her into the stone mouth, allowing it to devour me.

Inside, the smell of the damp walls soaked into me, smothering me. My heart pounded in my throat. I clung to the light that trickled through the opening, frozen within its tiny borders.

Eloise tugged at me, prompting me to follow her.

Ahead, the high ceiling of the alcove narrowed to become little more than a tunnel. The others stood within its jaws, waiting to be swallowed. My mouth was dry; my heart throbbed in my ears; my body trembled; my fingers were locked on the stone walls.

"Dog say this way," Enon said firmly, swinging his massive arm, motioning me to follow.

"Go on ahead. I'm right behind you," I said, pointing down the tunnel with my chin.

"You follow Enon. I'll follow last," Bowen said, twisting his fist in my shirt and yanking me toward the head of the line.

I stumbled forward, gasping for air.

"Second wife," Bowen said with a sneer behind me and Saris punched him in the arm.

Bowen smiled broadly, rubbing his newly formed bruise.

"I would be proud to share this torch, Mr. Littlefield," the King said graciously.

"Thank you, Sire," I said, and gripped his cloak as if all our lives depended on it. He only smiled in return and followed Enon.

The ground, damp, mushy, strewn with small stones, sloped sharply as we followed its downward tread.

I turned my head to look over my shoulder as the last sliver of sunlight slipped from view. We were alone in the dark, working our way deeper into the bowels of the world.

My mind screamed, fought with itself, raced with the possibilities of the dark. All the horrible things that lay in wait for us; all the monsters dissolved in darkness, in the stone itself, ready to be reconstituted at our passing. I clung with equal fervor to the King's cloak and the flickering light from his torch.

At the head of the line, trotted the dog just beyond Enon and he at the very edge of the light. I could see little more than his feet as we rushed along the small tunnel.

My grip on the King's cloak strained as he tried to keep up with Enon. Eventually, I had to let go for fear of falling. They rushed ahead and I scurried behind to keep any part of my body in the light. I had convinced myself of its protection as long as it touched me, somewhere.

In the dark, time stood still. After what seemed like an eternity of racing about a series of tunnels, we stopped. Our present tunnel widened, becoming an alcove. For the first time since we left the surface we stood as a group instead of a line, all but the dog.

From this alcove, five new tunnels fanned out before us. I was happy for the chance to catch my breath and to stand under the light of both torches.

Having shifted to be closer to the light I now had little idea from which tunnel we had come.

We stood silently and waited. The sounds of the dog snuffling down one of the tunnels meant he was making his way back. Suddenly, he appeared only to choose another tunnel and disappear again.

We waited until all sounds of him evaporated into the dark.

No one spoke, only the sputtering of the torches accompanied us. Eventually, Noget returned only to repeat the ritual down another tunnel. He did so again and again until all had been explored. At last he returned to sit in front of Enon. Even in this light, his face was clearly twisted in anguish. Eloise could see it as well.

"Well? Where is she?" She asked, sliding her hand into his.

"Dog say Izie... here... here... here," he said flatly, pointing to several of the tunnels.

"She can't be in all of them," I said, without thinking.

"She's passed through them at one time or another," the King said, placing his hand on my shoulder.

"What do we do now?" I asked, knowing what the answer would be.

"We split up," Bowen said through clenched teeth.

"Enon, dog go this one," he said and ran head long into a tunnel, the dog trotting by his side.

"He doesn't have a torch," I gasped.

"He's not afraid of the dark," Bowen snapped. He stood for a moment and then softly said something in Jonda to Saris, holding his hand out to her.

She folded her arms and turned from him in response. He grabbed the torch from her and headed down the next tunnel in line.

"I'm not afraid of the dark. All I said was Enon doesn't have a torch. That's all," I yelled angrily after him. I turned to the perplexed faces of the others. "It's the Norha I'm afraid of," I said half to myself, half to them.

"I guess this one's ours," the King said with far more joviality than I liked. He stood at the entrance of the third in line, bowing slightly and waved his arm as if in welcome. I stood motionless waiting for someone, anyone to go first. Eloise's eyes narrowed, cutting me to the core.

"It just gets better and better," I said and took a small step into the next ring of hell.

This tunnel was smaller than the first. I had to crouch slightly, cautiously running my hands along the damp walls as I stepped deeper inside. The walls were almost smooth, rippled in places. It was as if I was feeling the ribs of a great beast frozen in a gaping yawn. Eloise followed next, then the King, and then Saris.

We inched our way down as the tunnel twisted and turned in every imaginable direction. It became larger for a few steps and then smaller again.

We followed its path to what we thought was near the end, but it split again becoming three more.

My heart sank with the fear of being lost in the tunnels forever, or at least, until the Norha found us. I was confident we could follow this one back to its beginning and Goddess willing, find the one to the outside.

I turned to the others, ready to argue my point. As I did, the King held up his hand to silence me before I could say a word. He cocked his head, listening. Everyone followed his lead. We were frozen in place, waiting for whatever it was he heard to repeat itself.

My heart pounded in my ears. I was certain what the King heard was the Norha; it came again, soft, low, echoing effortlessly off the passageway walls.

"Again," the voice said, barely audible.

We spun to the mouth of each passageway, Eloise and I at the first, the King at the next and Saris at the last, hoping to hear it again.

Time slowed, stretching to heartbeats. Murmurs of speech trickled to us. We shifted, trying for a better advantage.

"Again," came the voice, louder this time. It was enough for all to hear.

Saris motioned us to follow before she dove into the passage, quickly disappearing.

I rushed to join the others, last in the line of descent.

Our path plunged steeply, making it difficult to hold my footing. The torch had been all but forgotten. A dull orange light filled the tunnel from the other end.

At its open end, it widened to become something akin to a parapet. It was as if our path had flung itself out beyond its confines and hung in midair, projecting into an enormous cavern. A low wall framed the end of this torrent of stone frozen in place.

From beyond this overhang, the voice was loud and clear. We lay on our stomachs and inched our way to look over the edge.

"Again," the voice demanded angrily, echoing throughout the grotto. Some twenty feet below, a small army of Norha formed a circle, at its center, next to a meager fire, stood Kathryn, her back to us.

"I can't."

"Again," Kathryn shouted, her voice distorted by the echo. She shifted her body, revealing Elizabeth. "Do it," she yelled reaching out to slap the child. The sound of it was sharp, crisp.

It stirred me with anger.

Eloise's body jerked in reaction. The King quickly placed his hand over her mouth to halt any outcry.

The child stiffened, wiping angry tears defiantly from her face. She held her hands out in front of her as Kathryn stepped back.

Slowly, a chant, no more than a whisper, escaped Elizabeth's lips. It grew faster, louder as she bent to scoop a handful of soil. She held it high as the words poured from her. Her expression was angry, full of hatred and locked on Kathryn.

She moved to the fire, and it jumped in response to her. She called to it as it belched high into the air. A large piece of it broke free and hovered in the air, spinning faster and faster to become a ball. She held out her free hand and the fire obeyed like a trained bird, spinning wildly in the palm of her hand. Her voice almost cracked as it reached a fevered pitch. Suddenly, she slammed her hands together. A small bolt of lightning escaped from her as her hands met. The cavern boomed with the sound of thunder, vibrating to the very core of me.

There at her feet, forged from the fire, shaped from the soil she held, sat a rabbit. To my shock it was alive.

"Good, Sister, good," Kathryn applauded.

Elizabeth looked tired, spent as if the creation took more from her than she had to give.

Kathryn bent to inspect the new arrival.

"Ow. The little bastard bit me," she cried, yanking away her hand.

"He doesn't like you," Elizabeth hissed through clenched teeth. Her face was an open book of her true feelings.

"You are no match for me, Sister. Remember this," Kathryn said, reading the child's face.

She lifted a heavy foot and stomped the small creature. Instantly, it became nothing more than sand and a modest puff of flame.

Elizabeth, hardly able to lift her arms, stood with an obvious defiance.

"Sister," Kathryn said, moving closer to her student with a serpentine ease.

The child stood fast, folding her arms.

Kathryn made a wide circle around her, fidgeting with something in her pocket. Moving in front of the child, she crouched, holding something in her hand. She unfolded it, inches from Elizabeth's face.

"Do you know what this is?" she cooed, holding it out by one end. There between her fingers, dangling from a corner was a piece of torn cloth, heavily stained with blood. Elizabeth's defiant face dropped, only to be replaced with shock, confusion, and a horrible sense of recognition.

"Yes," she said as if surrendering, taking the scrap. "It's Nana's."

"The Norha are not that discriminating. It's all that's left of her," her voice dropped lower, more malevolent. "What a pity, such a waste. I hear your mother isn't well."

The defiant expression returned to Elizabeth's face as she dropped the scrap of cloth and spit on the ground.

"If you fail me, Sister," Kathryn said sternly, slapping her once more.

"Monster!" Eloise screamed, jumping to her feet, pitching our torch over the edge at her. "I'm here, child. We've come for you."

"Nana!" Elizabeth screamed.

Kathryn grabbed her by the arm, almost lifting her off the ground, cursing. I pulled at Eloise. She stood transfixed, locked eye to eye with Kathryn.

The cavern instantly filled with the angry voices of the Norha. They were everywhere, charging into the tunnels, scaling the walls, anything to reach us.

We ran, darting back into the tunnels. It didn't take long to realize we had chosen the wrong one, Saris was nowhere to be seen, she had taken another. We were lost.

The King, sword drawn, hung back briefly. He cocked his head to the side, turning slightly, listening. Amid the many sounds bouncing off the walls, hidden among the voices of the Norha, one voice raised slightly above all others... Grimwell. He was somewhere in the tunnels driving the Norha.

"Sire, this way," Eloise called to the King as we darted into yet another passage.

He stood transfixed, refusing to follow. He was locked onto that voice. He turned slowly as if looking through the stone walls, searching for Grimwell.

"Sire, please," Eloise pleaded.

I stood at the opening, dreading the darkness ahead and the fear of the Norha behind us.

"Go. Find Elizabeth," he ordered, balancing the sword in his hand, his jaw muscle flexed intently, his teeth grinding together.

"Sire!" Eloise cried. But he was gone, disappearing into the corridor beyond.

"This way," I said, taking her hand, pulling her with me.

The King's voice echoed through the tunnels as he called to Grimwell.

The fingers of stone opened and closed in rips and gouges from top to bottom like pickets in a fence. Flashes of the King appeared briefly before disappearing again. We ran along a parallel passageway to that of the King's, we on an upper level, he running along the lower. The voices of the Norha echoed off the walls in every direction. It was difficult to tell how close they truly were. The voices grew in volume and excitement. The King had been spotted and the Norha gave chase in earnest.

My heart pounded as the voices drew closer. I tried to decide which way to go. My desire to stay in the light was torn by the real danger of the Norha. I pulled in one direction and Eloise in the other.

"This way," I said with open irritation.

"No, he's over this way," she said, yanking me toward her.

Eloise and I froze in place. I couldn't hear the words, just the voices. The first belonged to the King and the other to Grimwell.

We followed the sounds, as they became angrier.

We raced along the path as it rose. It ended in a small circle of stones, a dead-end, overlooking a smaller path below. Grimwell and the King were close. Their voices rang out clearly.

Suddenly, the King stumbled into the clearing below, knocked to the ground. Grimwell followed immediately, sword in hand. He swung it with madness. Stabbing at the King, he drove it into the ground where His Majesty had been but a breath before. His face twisted with a derangement I had seen only once in my life.

Again and again he stabbed as the King rolled just beyond his reach, until his sword found its target. The King screamed in agony as the thin steel bore through his upper thigh and his blood ran freely. Eloise cried out, half covering her mouth with one hand and the other trembling, outstretched toward the King. Grimwell looked up to see us for the first time.

"Say goodbye to the old King," he roared, now standing over the King. A wicked smile of self-satisfaction curled the corner of his lips. He drew back, gathered all his strength and plunged the sword.

Eloise screamed and turned her face into my shoulder.

The King rolled away knocking Grimwell over with his legs.

With the force of Grimwell's hate, the sword broke as it struck the rock where the King had lain.

Throwing the broken hilt to the ground, Grimwell picked up a large jagged rock in its replacement. He dove upon the King, trying to sit on his chest. He held the stone with both hands high over his head. His face was full of insanity. His eyes bulged, threatening to fall out of his head.

The King pushed, enraged, forcing Grimwell to the ground at his feet. Both men, as well as the ground, were covered in his blood. The chamber shook with Grimwell's growl of anger and he rose again, lifting the stone with a ferocious scream. He brought it down in a savage blow. Time slowed as the stone came crashing down, crushing the King's lower leg.

Eloise's body jerked against mine with his scream and the sickening snap of bone. She pushed her face deeper into my shoulder and sobbed.

The King pushed weakly against the ground in retreat. His leg, now folded outward away from his body, bled profusely.

Grimwell slowly pulled himself up to sit on the King's chest, striking him in the face. The King fought to remain conscious but had little strength left to lift his arms.

Grimwell lifted the stone once more. As he rocked back, his hands held it high over his head, his chest exposed.

I had to do something. Pushing past Eloise, I pulled the dagger, the King's gift to me, from my boot.

"Bastard," I yelled and flung it with all the strength I had to bear. I put all my will into its throwing, praying it would find its mark. It droned through the air, glinting in the torch light spinning end for end. I held my breath, waiting for it to strike.

As he rose... it struck him... hilt-first and then fell harmlessly to the ground.

Grimwell looked down at his chest and laughed a madman's laugh. It echoed through every part of the cavern ever more insanely.

"No!" Enon said, suddenly there. He stood behind Grimwell, grabbing the Chancellor's wrist. Grimwell's strength, rooted in his insanity nearly matched Enon's. The two struggled, tugging against each other.

The King, his hand hidden from my view, fumbled weakly about the floor. Somehow he found the dagger, raised it and plunged it into Grimwell's exposed chest.

Grimwell froze, releasing the rock to Enon. Slowly, his hands slipped to the King's throat.

The King made no effort to stop him but simply slid the dagger a second time between his ribs.

Enon sent the back of his huge hand to Grimwell's head, knocking him lifelessly to the ground.

"Hurt good," Enon said, looking up toward us.

As he cradled the King in his arms, Eloise and I climbed down from our perch to join them. Bowen and Saris found us shortly after that.

"You old fool," Eloise admonished as she slipped to the ground next to the King.

"Charming, as always," he grimaced.

She tore a piece of clothing to tie off his bleeding.

"I think this belongs to you," he said weakly, handing me the bloody dagger.

"You have to get him out of here," I said, looking deep into Eloise's eyes.

"We all go together," she insisted, uncertainty, doubt and fear crossing her face.

"No. Enon find Izie," Enon said, standing.

"We," she started again.

"No," Enon said stiffly.

"Wife, I can't do what I have to do if I'm worried about you," I said sternly, placing my hand on hers.

"You said wife," she said softly.

"I might have. I'm under a lot of pressure here. You have to go. I have to know you're safe."

"Tucker," she started.

I placed my hand to her lips to stop her.

"Take the King, take her," I said to Bowen now there, nodding toward Eloise. "You have to go. Enon and I will find Elizabeth and then we'll find you. Now get out of here."

Saris looked to me and then to Bowen.

Bowen's expression darted between Saris and me.

"First wife," Bowen said, looking deep into her eyes.

"First wife," she repeated and then kissed him, with a big smile.

The King groaned in pain as they pulled him up, spreading his arms over their shoulders. Eloise glanced back at me, her face bathed in tears, her bottom lip quivering. It was the longest goodbye I could ever remember.

Slowly, I stood, watching them until they were out of sight, praying I would see them again.

Chapter 15

Enon and I stared after them. My heart sank as the sound of each footfall faded, swallowed by the darkness. We were alone.

Behind us, the clamoring sounds of the Norha grew closer.

Enon turned to me and smiled.

"Brother, Dog say Izie this way," he said, laying a heavy hand on my shoulder.

"Enon," I said, trying to sound brave.

"Enon scared also. Tucker Soul-Bearer, protect Enon. Enon not so scared."

The idea of my being his protector struck us both funny and we laughed. I wasn't so frightened after that.

We stood waiting. I wasn't sure why at first, and then the Norha turned the corner and we ran, leading them away from the others.

Noget charged from path to path and we followed with total faith. We ducked into a steep tunnel, sliding to its bottom and waited.

The Norha raced beyond our hiding place and we moved on.

The dog snorted at the ground repeatedly, hesitating briefly and then ran ahead again.

Eventually, we stumbled upon another small alcove. In the back wall, was a small slit cut through the stone from floor to ceiling. A dull orange, flickering glow of light pushed greedily at its edges. The dog sat motionless for a moment, as if trying to decide something. It turned its large head toward Enon, blinked several times and then, I swear, smiled. Without a word from Enon, it charged into the fissure, disappearing from sight.

Enon followed, pushing his way through the crevice, forcing the opening to become slightly larger. On the other side, a huge chamber arched high into the darkness. He waited for a moment, held in awe by the scene in front of us.

As far as the eye could see, stretched a lake of melted stone; the smell of it burned my lungs.

I didn't want to follow. Looking through the gap between his body and his arm, I could see more than I wanted, more than I dared.

The air was on fire, burning in great bursts of orange and yellows. Massive swirls of flame danced wildly everywhere. Individual fragments of the liquid stone flew in enormous swarms, bouncing off the cavern walls, changing direction like a flock of birds. Their fiery tails faded as they fell back into the molten lake, only to be launched into the air once more. The ground moaned deep inside the world and a thousand shards took flight again. More of the rock erupted, splashing high against the cavern walls, washing down in a dull orange rumbling glow.

I shook inside. I had followed him through the darkness hoping to discover a safe haven, only to descend into hell itself.

"Izie," he screamed, half pulling me along, half running.

Beyond all rational thought, the dark silhouette of Kathryn and the child stood out against the burning gleam of melted stone. At the edge of this molten lake, Kathryn waved her hand, bringing down a bolt of lightning. It drove itself deep into the liquid rock close to them and the stone rose like a serpent. Slowly, it undulated, rising to do her bidding.

The material, deep amber orange in color, roiled under its weight, torn between its nature and her command. Slowly, compelled in this manner, great roundish globs of glowing stone forced themselves to the surface. One under the other, growing larger with each passing moment, they crested like the head of a wave. In their path, crisscrossed with a bright blue ash, they pushed out deeper into the lake. They rippled and arced upward, pulling to new heights, stretching out to become a bridge. The surface darkened to a deep translucent blue, as if suddenly becoming water and Kathryn, with Elizabeth in tow, stepped out, following the transformation. The fiery lake churned more wildly than before as the bridge snaked its way to the center. The molten rock splashed against the newly formed walls like waves beating on an unrelenting cliff.

"Izie!" Enon screamed, threading his way past stone outcroppings, forcing his way to the bridge, the dog ever at his side.

I followed for fear of being left behind to the Norha, stepping where he had stepped. Before I could form a rational thought, I stood where the bridge had rooted itself in the stone bank.

The blue ash paved the surface in thin trails, twisting and changing below my feet like trickling water. Between them, the dull orange glow of liquid stone pulsed with a life of its own under the surface.

Enon raced ahead, running along the newly formed pavement to reach Elizabeth. I stood frozen at the edge of solid ground and the path taken by Enon. I couldn't force myself to venture beyond this vestige of safety.

"Stop him, Sister. Stop him, or I will kill him myself," Kathryn growled, her voice echoing, filling the cavern.

"Father," the child's voice pierced all other sounds, stabbing deep into my heart.

I found myself pulled onto the bridge by her cries and, before I realized it, I kept pace just behind Enon once more.

"Izie!" Enon roared, rushing toward the child.

"Stop him, Sister, I warn you," Kathryn spit, holding the child roughly by her wrist.

Elizabeth looked into her eyes and believed the threat. She hung her head for a moment before looking to Enon. He and the dog approached, stopping just beyond arm's reach.

"Forgive me, Father," she said softly. She pulled free of Kathryn's grip. Closing her eyes, she tilted back her head. Slowly, her arms drifted upward. Her lips moved quickly as she whispered softly to herself.

The trails of rippling blue ash swirled at her feet, gathering speed and mass. It rose slowly, becoming taller, wider, like dust caught in a devil's wind.

Enon stepped cautiously backward.

"I'm sorry," Elizabeth said, opening her eyes. She clapped her hands. Instantly, a small bolt of lightning struck the swirling ash, sending it into a wall of blue flame, jumping high into the air and cutting a rift no more than a foot wide through the newly formed pavement, boring deep into the molten lake. It formed a wall dividing us, we on one side and they on the other. It burned with an intensity that shook me to the very core.

Enon peered through the translucent barrier in dismay.

Satisfied, Kathryn pushed the child to the edge to pursue her conjuring, calling to the lake. Shielded by the small body of the child, she laid a hand on Elizabeth's shoulder and began to cast her spell.

She screamed unintelligible words, commanding bolt after bolt to join with her. Each struck with blinding power and fierce energy. It pulsed through her body, coursing down her arm in large glowing bursts, filling the youth. It leapt from Elizabeth's outstretched hands, more powerful than in its beginning. The child screamed in horrible pain, arcing backwards as it passed through her to the lake below.

In response, the molten stone exploded into the air more wildly than before, sending volumes of the material everywhere. The wall of blue flame acted as a barrier, shielding us from the fiery rain. The ground shook with unbelievable violence and the molten stone flew in greater swarms above us. I huddled near Enon under the umbrella of certain death.

The glowing stone oozed down the face of the translucent walls, inching their way down to the pool once more. Enon was unmoved.

Kathryn's words summoned something from the bottom.

Drawn from within the center of this burning hell, three objects, each twice the size of a man's fist, glowed with a pulsating blue light.

Freed from their fiery berth, great fingers of lightening crackled fiercely between the objects and Elizabeth as they lifted higher into the air. They floated, held in place by the power that Kathryn wielded, withering the child.

"Izie!" Enon shouted, reaching out toward her. Too close to the wall of blue flame, his sleeve caught fire. He ripped it from his body, throwing it over the side. His flesh, burnt a savage red, dripped openly with blood.

My heart became a lump in my throat as the dog paced anxiously in front of the wall of blue flames, waiting for what came next. The veins in Enon's neck pounded under his flesh, flushing a deep red. He threw back his head and roared with anger, a savagery I had not seen in him before this moment.

"Izie!" he screamed and plunged his fist through the curtain of flame.

"Father!" Elizabeth screamed in return, trying to break free of Kathryn's hold.

I reached out for Enon, trying to pull him back to safety. The ground rumbled from deep below me and all the energy that could flow through me suddenly was in my possession. The symbols in the palm of my hand jumped to life again, bathing him in blue light. I struggled to hold on, passing the healing energy to him, giving him what little protection I had to offer.

He roared in unimaginable pain but refused to remove his arm from the flame.

"True heart, Father here," he screamed in agonizing torrents.

"Go, save yourself. She will kill you," Elizabeth cried, turning her tearful face to him.

"Without only child... father already dead," he said in little more than a whisper, turning up his palm, pleading to her.

Elizabeth extended her hand toward him in response.

"Give up, Citizen. You are no match for me," Kathryn said, her voice full of the insanity of this place. She spun to throw a bolt of energy in our direction.

Fear ripped through every fiber of my body. She was right. I was no match for her.

I struggled to hold on.

"But I am," came a voice from behind me.

I turned to see Daneba as she released several bolts of lightning of her own. They sheared through the curtain of blue flames to strike Kathryn full in the chest. Kathryn reeled momentarily, releasing the child. The glowing stones dropped back into the lake, and the curtain disappeared, no longer a threat.

Enon fell forward as Elizabeth rushed to him.

I collapsed where I stood, pushing hard against the pavement.

"You've ruined it. You've ruined it all!" Kathryn screeched, her face contorted, twisted with insanity. She sent a sizzling bolt toward Daneba, who deflected it and sent one in return.

"Go. Go now!" Daneba yelled over her shoulder in our direction as she advanced on Kathryn.

I didn't wait for a second invitation.

Enon scooped up Elizabeth in his arms and ran.

It was all I could do to keep up with him and the dog.

Behind us, Daneba and Kathryn battled with torrents of lightning and melted stone. The bridge had begun to suffer, coming apart, returning to its former self. We ran for all we were worth. On the shore of stone ahead of us, a handful of the Norha had begun to gather.

Noget, first to reach this safety, charged headlong into them. They beat at the dog with sticks and he routed them, clearing a path before us.

I raised my hand and the symbols glowed. The Norha covered their faces with their arms and cried in angry fear. Their hands grabbed, clutching at my clothes as we passed. I blindly followed Enon's lead, hoping only to escape before running out of breath. The angry voices of the Norha gave chase and sticks and stones pelted us in our retreat.

From the many tunnels that emptied into this cavern, more Norha joined the first, more of them and more still, too many to be intimidated by me. I glanced over my shoulder as a seemingly uncountable number of them now followed our escape. In the distance, the cries from Daneba and Kathryn's pitched battle filled the air. Thunder exploded, shaking everything, sending small stones cascading down the walls. It had begun to rain red-hot globules of melted stone, painting the walls with its fire.

Behind us, the Norha were coming. It was obvious to all of us that there was nowhere left to go. We charged headlong into the nearest tunnel, into the dark. Only the burning rain behind us lighted the way. We twisted and turned until I was lost beyond hope. The tunnel became darker and darker, but even here Enon seemed to know where to go. I found myself slowing for fear of the darkness and then rushed forward to be closer to the safety of Enon.

We followed the moist walls until they went no farther, eventually ending. They widened out, not becoming a room, but more than a tunnel, a hollow in the shadows.

In the faint trickle of light that forged ahead of the Norha torches, Enon fumbled at the walls.

He wedged his huge arm behind the timbers framing the mouth of our dead end. The timber groaned as he placed one foot against the wall and shoved.

The groan became a wooden wail and timbers holding this end of the shaft open failed, crashing in with a cloud of dirt, dust and stone, trapping us inside.

The Norha found us as the last of the stone fell, blocking all but a small opening of the doorway. Their arms and hands shot through every hole and crevice, waving wildly. They pushed, shoved and climbed over one another to get through the small opening to reach us, intent on the child.

I looked about quickly. To my disappointment, Noget was no where to be seen; on this side of the barricade was only Enon, Elizabeth and myself.

On the other side, the Norha pulled at the stones. They would dig through to us at any moment. As the thought entered my mind, one of them wriggled through and then a second, followed quickly by a third.

"No," I screamed and held my hand out toward them.

The energy burst from me, bathing the opening in white light. It rippled up from the ground, stirring my insides, advancing to burst into the physical world from my outstretched hand.

The first of the Norha to be caught in its shimmer threw their hands over their faces and screamed in unholy agony. Their flesh ripped from their bodies in small pieces, torn from them as leaves from a tree in winter. For a moment, their skeletons, driven forward by those behind, continued to advance upon us before falling to the ground, little more than dust.

That dark part of them that passed as a soul swirled about the grotto and then plunged into my chest. As more and more of them perished their souls, gathered in this manner, sickened me. My stomach pitched and churned horribly before a dark, thick puke vaulted out of my mouth.

The Norha fell back and the energy faded.

"Father love... always," Enon said, kissing Elizabeth's forehead and pushing her into my arms. I strained to see what was happening.

He grabbed a large ceiling beam and pushed. At first, nothing happened and then a second try and it groaned. Dirt and small stones began to fall. A third effort and the beam groaned loudly and dirt poured freely in on top of us. Again, with a brutal shove a small opening appeared.

A beam of light stabbed through the darkness. It was small, no more than the width of a chair leg. Dust hung in the air, dancing in its length, making it appear almost solid.

Out of reflex or instinct, I reached up for the thin line of light as if it were a rope rooted in salvation, a rope that reached into the very bottom of this hell.

The symbols in my palm jumped to life once more. An explosion of energy leapt from my hand, tracing the path of light back to the surface. The dirt shifted, raining down on us and the light blinked in and out of existence.

The Norha charged forward and through the hail of dirt their hands pulled at me.

The small room suddenly burst to life with brilliant sunlight. It washed over every corner of the chamber and the Norha recoiled with its unexpected appearance.

The shaft was now several feet across and opened to blue sky above.

"Now, Brother," Enon yelled.

To my shock, the dog began to appear, pulling itself, materializing from the center of Enon's chest. Fully formed, it fell to the floor, turning to look at me before leaping to the opening. With Elizabeth tucked under my arm I followed its lead and grabbed the dog's tail. The beast yanked me forward and pulled with the strength of several men, racing to the surface.

The dirt shifted as if the newly created tunnel was trying to close upon us. The roots hung out of the walls like greedy fingers, grabbing at us, holding us, trying to bind us. As the walls began to close, becoming smaller, the fear of being buried alive flooded my mind. My heart pumped with an unnatural strength, with true fear. The musky smell of dirt filled my lungs. I couldn't breathe. The roots behind pulled at me and those ahead snatched at Elizabeth, trying to separate us. I held her all the tighter. My hand slipped down the length of the dog's tail. It moved ahead without looking back, focused on the small blue spot in the distance. Nothing stopped it, not the roots ripping at us, nor the shifting dirt under our feet, not the angry voices of the Norha gathering below us. The three of us exploded into the sunlight, bathed in fresh air. The child and I tumbled to the grassy ground, free of that dark hell.

The dog stood, its feet spread wide, its head held low. Its body heaved as it fought to catch its breath. It stared into my eyes for a moment and then plunged into the collapsing tunnel.

I lurched head first after the animal, grasping in vain at the air behind him. There, bathed in the shaft of light at the bottom stood Enon, still holding the ceiling beam. The Norha clung to him, all but obscuring him, covering him like devouring maggots.

I watched in disbelief as the dog, driven by madness, releasing a snarl of pure anguish, raced down the shaft and dove headlong into Enon's chest. Suddenly, it was as if one or both had become liquid and they melted one into the other and Enon rose a little taller, a little stronger.

At that moment, I understood his mother's last wish. There was only one soul, divided, shared between man and beast, never to be alone.

Strengthened by this joining, Enon looked up at me, his eyes piercing mine, as a broad smile slowly spread over his face.

"Cayra, Brother," he called to me... then let go of the beam.

The hole instantly filled in, flooding the cavern below, burying one and all alive.

A plume of dust belched from the hole, rising high into the air, covering everything. Soil continued to pour in on top of them like sand emptying from an hourglass.

"Father!" Elizabeth screamed as we dug in vain with our hands. We dug until our fingers became raw and bloody and we could dig no more.

Time slowed. Our efforts, our hearts, our hopes lay buried at the bottom of this shaft.

"We have to go," I said softly, smoothing her hair. "We're not safe here."

"We can't leave him. You can't just let him die!" she screamed at me.

"I'm sorry, Princess," I said, wiping the tears from my eyes.

"I won't go," she sobbed and began to dig even more frantically.

I got to my feet and picked her up. She kicked and screamed and beat at me as I laid her over my shoulder and started down the mountain.

"I HATE YOU. I HATE YOU..."

****

The tavern door suddenly swung open with a sharp bang against the wall. The images floating over head evaporated instantly and everyone turned toward the door.

"Tucker Littlefield, there's work to be done and here you sit with your drunken friends. Am I supposed to sit at home and wait until you stumble home to cut firewood?"

"Ah, everyone, my lovely wife Eloise," I said with a modest bow and wave of my hand.

She stood in the center of the tavern door, her foot wedged to hold it open, and her hands on her hips. Her face was flushed red and her lips were pursed.

"I was just on my way and stopped for but a moment to bring home a little something for dessert. When these fine people asked if I was the lucky individual married to the fearless Eloise Littlefield they had heard so much about. I, of course... "

"Save your lies for someone who believes them. I can smell your breath from here. I know how long it takes to fill a room this size with the stench of your tobacco, Tucker Littlefield, so not another word. The firewood won't cut and stack itself."

"I was just on the way, my love," I said and slipped down from the table.

Nearly all present stood to leave, speaking happily to one another. Many gave me a pat on my shoulder, as well as a generous smile and nod as they passed.

"One last thing, friends, before we all go home as good men of family, as his soul-bearer, I would know, I would feel his passing. He is, forgive me, he must still be alive. Has anyone seen or heard of Enon Tutelo before this night?" I asked; hope swelling large in my chest.

No one spoke.

The crush of disappointment must have been easy to read on my face.

"Come along, husband. You promised to repair the gate and morning comes quickly," Eloise said softly, holding out her hand to me.

"Here we are, friend. A bargain is a bargain," my patron said and handed me the leather bag that had been placed on the table for safekeeping.

He opened the bag and allowed it to drop to the table once more with a good deal of commotion. He slipped his hand into his pocket, retrieving several coins more and made a show of putting them in the bag. They made a considerable noise as they dropped among the others. "A true bargain, indeed," he said loudly.

Many of the others followed his lead and as the last pushed past Eloise to leave, the bag had reached overflowing.

Eloise and I now stood alone.

"Why do you do that? The King has been most generous," she asked, shaking her head at me.

"A man wants to pay his own way, my love," I answered with pride. "Jack, if you please," I said as he entered, nodding toward the bag.

"With pleasure, old friend. You will come by tomorrow to divvy up, of course?" he asked, giving the bag a playful shake.

Eloise gave me a distasteful look.

"My good man, what are you thinking? I am a family man and would rather cut off my own foot and eat it than be separated from my loving household. Now, if you don't mind, my dessert." I smiled broadly.

Jack turned his head in Eloise's direction and jiggled the bag.

She rolled her eyes and flung open the door, and waited.

I followed quickly. After all, it was dark outside.

"Tomorrow, then," he called after us as the door slowly swung closed.

We walked toward home in silence for a few moments.

"I am sorry. I was certain you would have heard something this time," she said at last, smoothing her hand over my back.

"As did I... seven townships this time."

"Really? Seven?" she countered.
"Seven."
"Well, then."

Her hand was warm, comforting on my back. We walked the remainder of the way to our gate without a word.

"Did you hear that?" she asked as she swung the gate open.

"Hear what?" I asked, turning to the darkness.

"I thought I heard a dog."

"I didn't hear anything," I admonished softly.

"Listen," she insisted.

Somewhere in the darkness behind us, somewhere close by, the sounds of a dog, a very large dog, padded through the dry leaves. For a moment I thought...

I leaned out and then a step, perhaps two, maybe a few more, expecting to see... I'm not sure what. I stood, waiting for the sound to show itself, but it did not. Only the night breeze answered my desire.

"Husband, morning comes quickly," Eloise said, drawing me back.

I stared into the endless night for a moment or two before nodding in silent agreement. She smoothed her hand over my shoulder as I made my way into the house.

She stood for a moment, listening, peering out into the darkness before closing the gate behind us.

Tomorrow would be another day... perhaps this time... Big fish... little fish, one never knew.

CPSIA information can be obtained at www.ICGtesting.com
Printed in the USA
LVOW132330241112

308666LV00005B/844/P